THEO STRODE QUICKLY THROUGH THE WOODS. Already his legs were aching from the unaccustomed exercise. But it was a nice ache, not the horrible pain that followed his treatment.

Suddenly he saw it. Under the glistening leaves of a thick holly tree, a tiny parcel was perched on top of a gravestone. It was wrapped in black paper, with a golden bow tied around it. Tiny beads of rain shone on the bow.

He looked closer. Written in silver ink on the black paper was one word: *Theo*.

*Theo sat up and looked around. He saw a glowing candle on a tombstone in front of him. Suddenly a dark figure stepped in front of it.*

# CANDLE MAN

## BOOK ONE

## THE SOCIETY OF UNRELENTING VIGILANCE

GLENN DAKIN

**EGMONT**

USA

*New York*

To Sara and Cory — *my* secret society

◆■◆

EGMONT
*We bring stories to life*

First published by Egmont USA, 2009
This paperback edition published by Egmont USA, 2010
443 Park Avenue South, Suite 806, New York, NY 10016

Copyright © Glenn Dakin, 2009
Illustrations copyright © Greg Swearingen, 2009
All rights reserved

1 3 5 7 9 8 6 4 2

www.egmontusa.com
www.glenndakin.com

THE LIBRARY OF CONGRESS HAS CATALOGED THE HARDCOVER EDITION AS FOLLOWS:
Dakin, Glenn.
The Society of Unrelenting Vigilance / Glenn Dakin ;
[illustrations by Greg Swearingen].
p. cm. — (Candle Man ; bk. 1)
Summary: Thirteen-year-old Theo, who has lived in seclusion his entire life,
discovers he is the descendant of the Candle Man, a Victorian vigilante with
the ability to melt criminals with a single touch.
ISBN 978-1-60684-015-3 (trade hardcover) — ISBN 978-1-60684-047-4
(reinforced lib. bdg. ed.) [1. Adventure and adventurers—Fiction.
2. Superheroes—Fiction.] I. Swearingen, Greg, date–. ill. II. Title.
PZ7.D152225So 2009
[Fic]—dc22
2009014035
Paperback ISBN 978-1-60684-136-5

Printed in the United States of America

CPSIA tracking label information:
Random House Production · 1745 Broadway · New York, NY 10019

# ACKNOWLEDGMENTS

The author would like to thank Alice Barker
and Rachel Boden at Egmont UK,
as well as Regina Griffin at Egmont USA,
for their enthusiasm, insight, and vigilance
for Candle Man.

# Contents

# CHAPTER 1

# THE PRESENT

So THIS IS MY BIRTHDAY TREAT," Theo said, gazing about him. The teenager surveyed the world gloomily, the fine drizzle already causing his dark hair to droop over his unhappy gray eyes. "When you said I would be visiting a special place, surrounded by important people . . ."

"Just my little joke, young master," interrupted Mr. Nicely, Theo's butler, with a bright smile. The pair stood in a cemetery. Lopsided gravestones, monuments, and sad stone angels surrounded them. "There are a lot of important people in graveyards," the butler added.

Theo just looked miserable. His face was almost as pale as the marble cherubs in front of him. "I had hoped, now that I'm older . . . ," he began.

"Now, now"—Mr. Nicely wagged a finger—"you know you aren't safe amongst *living* people," he added, leading the way down a tangled path. "Or at least they aren't safe amongst you. On account of your condition."

"But I've got my gloves on," Theo protested, glancing down at the thick leather gauntlets he was ordered to wear at all times. He knew his words would be wasted. He was only too aware of the rules that governed his illness.

"Half an hour!" Mr. Nicely shouted, and twirled his umbrella jauntily.

Theo ignored the rain and peered around, his heart racing. He hadn't been out of the house for a year. He hadn't seen another person—outside of his household—for three hundred and sixty-five days. Theo's predictable routine meant he always saw the same three: Mr. Nicely the butler, Clarice the maid, and Dr. Emmanuel Saint, his guardian. No one else was allowed to enter his circle of misery. Just in case.

It would be a thrill simply to glimpse another human being.

2

"We might see someone — from a distance . . . ," Theo ventured.

"'Might' is not for you, young master," chuckled Mr. Nicely. "Your life has been planned and regulated to leave 'might' and 'maybe' out of the equation. Now take a quick stroll, enjoy the company of your betters" — here the butler nodded down at the leaf-strewn graves — "and we'll get back home."

Theo strode quickly through the woods. Already his legs were aching from the unaccustomed exercise. But it was a nice ache, not the horrible pain that followed his treatment. He peered through the clumps of thistles and old-man's beard that choked the pathways. Years ago his guardian had said a cemetery keeper lived here. There had been some mention of his having a daughter — maybe Theo would see them.

"I've half a mind to nip home early," the butler called out from somewhere behind him. Clearly Mr. Nicely had seen enough of this dreary November day already. "Then I can just squeeze in a nice cup of cocoa before the good doctor returns from his meeting."

*Home early? From my one trip out in three hundred and sixty-five days!*

Theo made an effort to distance himself from the

3

eternal presence of the butler. He ducked under the dark boughs of a knotty old hawthorn and found himself in a little clearing.

Suddenly he saw it. Under the glistening leaves of a thick holly tree, a tiny parcel was perched on top of a gravestone. It was wrapped in black paper, with a golden bow tied around it. Tiny beads of rain shone on the bow.

He looked closer. Written in silver ink on the black paper was one word: *Theo*. It was for him, only for him—somehow he knew not to mention it to his companion.

Too surprised to really know what he was doing, he slipped the little packet into his coat pocket. Then he turned around to see Mr. Nicely stroll into view.

"Come on." The butler grinned. "Early home, and a drop of cocoa for yours truly will be just the ticket. You've been far too unruly already!"

To the butler's surprise, Theo made no protest.

---

"Time to open your gifts!" Dr. Saint announced with a smile. His white teeth, round glasses, and bald head all gleamed down on Theo as he sat in the study. Theo was back at Empire Hall, the vast mansion in Kensington Gore—one of London's wealthiest quarters—where he and his guardian lived.

This was one of Theo's three rooms—the bathroom, his bedroom, and the study. He barely knew of any other places in the world. In front of him on a shiny walnut desk were three parcels, one from Dr. Saint, one from Mr. Nicely, and one from Clarice. They all waited expectantly.

Theo opened the gifts. The first was *The Complete Guide to Good Manners: Part Four,* a large volume from Dr. Saint. Then there was a framed photograph from Mr. Nicely—of himself. And finally, Clarice had bought Theo a book of fairy tales, ten years too young for him.

"Completely checked and approved by myself," Dr. Saint added, as Theo flicked through the book's garish illustrations.

He tried to say thank you, but his mouth only framed the words—no sound would come out.

"A bumper harvest," chortled Mr. Nicely.

Theo looked up. "But what about . . . ?"

"Yes?" demanded Dr. Saint.

"I asked for a book about the world, or about history—something about real life. . . ." He faltered.

Dr. Saint exchanged a glance with Mr. Nicely.

"I'm sorry, Theo," said Dr. Saint, eyeing his ward with a strange cold gaze. "But we've been through all this a hundred times. The world is not good for you and you are not good for it."

"So you keep saying!" Theo blurted out. "But I'm nearly a man now, and I haven't got a clue about what it's really like—out there!" He gestured towards the curtained window.

The doctor sighed and placed his hands together in the prayerlike gesture he often adopted when being wise.

"Now listen, Theobald. Facts about the world, real events, true history—all these things excite the mind. That stimulation is, sadly, very bad for you. It makes your mind race, your metabolism accelerate. The effect on your condition could be disastrous."

Theo looked away bleakly.

"I am trying to save you from your own curiosity, Theo," the doctor said. "I know that where a teenager is involved, I have set myself a thankless task!"

"You're a bloomin' hero, sir!" Mr. Nicely muttered, looking at the floor.

"But most of the time, I feel all right!" Theo cried out. "Apart from being bored out of my mind!"

Dr. Saint sighed. Mr. Nicely tutted.

"I fear Theo's thrilling day out has muddled his

wits," Dr. Saint said. "Warm up the Tube, Mr. Nicely. I suggest an extra-long session of therapy!"

Theo went pale.

That night, as on every other, he was forced to stand upright in the Mercy Tube, a transparent casing with a powerful ray emitter housed at the top. His eyes screwed tight against the blinding light, Theo was bathed in radiation for several minutes. He could hardly stand afterwards and felt sick in the pit of his stomach.

Clarice brought him a glass of water and his dressing gown. As he sat on the edge of his bed, he heard the others talking in the room next door.

"Well, I'm out with the Society of Good Works tonight," said Dr. Saint. "We have those widows to take care of, and a big check to give the prime minister."

"Very saintly of you, Dr. Saint," said Mr. Nicely.

"Nice of you to say so, Mr. Nicely," said Dr. Saint.

Theo grimaced, crawled up onto his bed half-dazed, and passed out.

It was evening. The thrum of traffic in the street was dying away. Unseen dogs exchanged barks farther down the Gore. Clarice came in to clear up the supper things. Theo leant back against his pillow and studied the halos of the lamplight on the ceiling.

He was pleased to be left alone with Clarice. With her plain face, short, mousy hair, and drab uniform, she couldn't be described as attractive, but she was a quiet, soothing presence. At least she didn't smile all the time.

"I've been thinking," Theo said. "If my condition is so bad, why don't I see anything wrong with my skin?" He peeled off his gloves as he always did before sleeping and studied his hands in the half light.

"And if the Mercy Tube is curing me—why do I only feel bad after I come out of it?" he continued, pleased to be able to ask questions freely. The maid picked up the tray and left the room without a word. It was all Theo had expected. After all, she was completely deaf.

At last Theo was alone. He stepped across the room, took the parcel from his coat pocket, and returned to his bed to study it. There was his name on the paper in ornate silver writing: *Theo*. He liked that. There was something about seeing his name written out in shiny letters by an unknown hand; it was as if *Theo* could be somebody special, a name to conjure with, not just a useless invalid.

He opened the present. Inside, packed in shredded paper, lay a snow globe. He had seen one or two of these before. The glass bowl contained a little miniature of Big Ben and the Houses of Parliament, a place he knew from one of his approved picture books. But there was no note with the gift, nothing to suggest who had sent it.

He shook the globe, expecting to see a swirl of white snow, a magical winter scene. But instead he stirred up a blizzard of black flakes. Theo watched in surprise as the dark shapes whirled like a cloud of bats above the tiny tower. As they settled, they blotted out the quaint scene, burying everything in darkness.

*Weird*, Theo thought. Frowning, he replaced the globe in his coat pocket and climbed into bed. He lay in the dark, wondering about the strange gift—and who could have sent it—until he drifted off to sleep.

His birthday had been more intriguing than he had expected. But he had no idea that the events of the night ahead would change his miserable life forever.

# CHAPTER 2

# THE SECRET ROOM

A SHATTERING OF GLASS WOKE THEO. He heard a rush of feet, somewhere far off in the mansion. He sat bolt upright in bed. Empire Hall was a smooth, well-regulated household—here, surprises and unexpected noises in the night were not tolerated.

Then came a sharp cry of pain from Mr. Nicely. Theo leapt out of bed. He could hear muffled arguing getting closer.

"You fool, Brady! You've gone and killed him!" whispered an old man.

"No, I ain't," snapped back a younger voice. "And there's no need to whisper either, Foley. We know there's just the two blokes living here, and we saw the other one go out."

A sudden rattling began at Theo's door. He stood, frozen in the shadows. "Look in here!" ordered the older voice. There was a splintering smash, and Theo's door flew open. In the half light from the hallway, Theo could make out a skinny old man in a long raincoat, and a big, younger man in a leather jacket. Theo stared, transfixed.

*People.*

The old man, Foley, had a haggard face with a tuft of ginger beard. Brady, the younger, had a clean-shaven head and a squashed nose.

"Blimey!" exclaimed Brady. "There's a kid in here!"

Theo froze as the two men advanced on him. The old one was smiling. He had horrible gray teeth, not perfect ones like Dr. Saint and Mr. Nicely. And he had spots and pimples all over his face. Theo found them very interesting.

"This is a piece of luck," said Foley. "Since you almost stiffed the butler, we need someone to show us around the house!"

"Oh, yeah," Brady said. "Someone to point us to the valuables!"

Foley waved a pistol at Theo.

11

"Is . . . is that for me?" asked Theo, wondering what the strange black metal object was.

"It *will* be for you, if you give us any lip!" snapped Brady.

Just in time, Theo remembered his Guide to Good Manners.

"I'm very sorry," he said quietly. "I don't believe we have been introduced."

The two men stared at him as if he had said something strange. Theo quickly asked the question he really wanted to ask.

"Would you mind telling me what you're doing here?"

The two men looked at each other. Brady suddenly raised a big ugly fist, covered in rings. Foley stopped him.

"Leave this to me. The boy's obviously a weirdy," Foley said, making a screwing gesture with his finger at the side of his head. "That must be why they keep him locked up in this room. And that's why we didn't know he lived here, even though you've been casing the job for two weeks!"

Foley turned back to Theo.

"Listen, kid," he said in his hoarse voice. "We're robbers. We've come to nick all the good stuff. So we need your help—as tour guide."

12

"Robbers." Theo nodded. "I know about you." He smiled, pleased with his worldly knowledge. "You're in one of my books of fairy tales. Ali Baba and the forty thieves." Theo looked around as if expecting another thirty-eight men to appear.

"Just show us where the loot is, and we won't have to crack your skull like we did to the butler."

"May I see?" asked Theo. The thought of Mr. Nicely with a cracked skull interested him strangely.

"No — he's in the hallway, tied up and gagged now, and *we're* calling the shots, not you, Weirdy. Now show us around the house."

Theo's face clouded over.

"I'm sorry," he sighed. "But I'm not really allowed out of my room."

Theo was shoved into the hallway, where he crashed into a grandfather clock and hurt his head.

"Nutter or not, a bit of old-fashioned persuasion will change your tune!" Brady snarled.

This physical pain after Theo's latest session in the Mercy Tube was making his head swim. He looked around the elegant oak-paneled hallway with wide eyes. He had hardly ever been in this part of the house before. A corridor led to several doorways at the end. What was down there? The kitchen? The garden? How he longed to see those places. But not with the robbers. Now he was scared.

"Upstairs," hissed Foley, and they made Theo stumble ahead of them as they mounted the long staircase. Suddenly Theo felt terribly anxious. He had never been upstairs before, and they expected him to show them around! Then Theo realized something else. . . .

"I—I'm not wearing my gloves!" he almost screamed.

Theo stared at his bare hands, and for a moment they seemed to stand out with strange clarity in the darkness. This fleeting impression soon vanished from his mind as the two men rounded on him.

"Shut it!" growled Brady, bunching a fist under Theo's chin.

"Listen, kid," Brady said, "we know you're crazy, but one more word—"

"You don't understand!" Theo said. "I have to wear my gloves, or—"

Now Foley jabbed the gun into Theo's ribs. "Enough!" he ordered. "Forget your rotten gloves! I know it's cold in this place, but one more squeak out of you—unless we tell you to speak—and you are dead."

Theo fell silent. He knew what dead meant.

Not long afterwards, Mr. Foley and Mr. Brady had cheered up. Theo had optimistically pointed them towards one of the rooms upstairs, and it had turned out to have some valuable gadgets, computers, and cameras in it. From the looks of it, this was Dr. Saint's bedroom. But the intruders soon started complaining again.

"Where's the real stuff?" Foley muttered. "This bloke Dr. Saint is the head of all sorts of charities. Gentlemen like that are always loaded. Sticky fingers, y'see."

"Show us more!" ordered Brady, shoving Theo ahead of them down the landing. Theo threw out a hand to steady himself, and he touched the head of a little statue of a nymph, set into a recess in the wall. To Theo's surprise, the statuette's head sank downwards into its body, followed by a sudden click and a low grinding noise.

A section of the wall slid back, revealing a concealed passage. All three stared in silence.

"Well done," breathed old Foley finally. "That's more like it."

A short, narrow passage led to a doorway, which was secured with a heavy lock and several bolts. There was a moment of professional reverence from the experienced burglars.

"We've hit the jackpot!" said Foley.

Theo watched, scared and fascinated as the two crooks set to work with a combination of sly know-how and crude violence. Screws were eased out, locks oiled and hammered, and the bolts studied and shattered. The thick inner door creaked open, revealing a dark chamber beyond. Using a tiny torch, Foley located a light switch. They stepped into the room, and Theo gazed around him, astonished.

*The forbidden things.* The room was littered with newspapers, magazines, photos—all the things that told you about *the real world*. Theo was not allowed to see such information. Dr. Saint had always told him that knowledge of real-life events, news, and history would only excite and confuse his mind.

But Theo could not help looking. Yellowing old newspaper articles were pinned to boards on the wall. There were maps of London, snapshots of crumpled bodies, pictures of sinister figures with strange names. Theo peered at the dark, illustrated image of a monstrous, misshapen man: *The Dodo,* a caption read.

"This can't be right. It's just a study or something . . . ," said Brady.

Unnoticed, Theo was looking through a pile of pictorial newspapers. He looked at the dates. They were over a hundred years old. There was so much to see, read, and drink in. . . .

*Crime Ring Broken by Unknown Crusader,* one magazine read. Another headline proclaimed: *New Hero of the Night* — but the picture with it had been removed.

Foley was staring about him, like a frightened rabbit. His teeth nibbled nervously on his lower lip.

"Well, say something, you old fool!" shouted Brady. Instead, Foley stepped towards a shadowy alcove at the far end of the room and switched on a lamp. They all stared. Theo's jaw dropped.

A pale, long-haired man in a smart cape was peering out at them from a sepia photograph in a golden frame. The man had a haunted, tragic face. Yet there was something strong and resolute in its lines too — the angular nose, tough chin, and those unfathomable eyes. Beneath the portrait was the legend: *The Candle Man.*

Theo stared. There was no mistake. For a moment time seemed to stand still. But there was no denying, his first startling impression had been correct. *The man in the picture looked exactly like Theo.*

"Candle Man? Never heard of him!" said Brady. "Have you?"

Foley nodded. "We should get out of here!" he whispered.

17

"What?"

"It's unlucky, you see . . ." Foley was almost as white as a sheet. "Especially in our game," the old man said. "It goes a long way back. People hear about the Candle Man, and not long after . . . they disappear."

"Then why haven't I heard of him?" Brady asked.

"It was all covered up—made into a secret. It was too horrible. . . ." The old man was distracted, ferreting around nervously at the piles of papers. He looked at some random photos and blanched.

"What a terrible way to go!" he gasped, putting the photos back facedown. He switched off the alcove light and tried frantically to replace everything they had touched.

"We've got to get out of here, now!" he urged. He was no longer the hardened housebreaker, but more like a terrified child. "This is way over our heads! We came to the wrong house tonight."

The old man headed straight out of the room, and Brady followed.

"This is crazy! Get a grip!" the younger man roared, but Foley was bounding down the stairs now with a speed hard to believe for his age. Brady was slower, dragging Theo by the arm. In the downstairs hallway, Foley turned to stare at Theo.

"We're in dark waters," Foley said. "No one must know we've been here!"

"That means offing the boy!" shouted Brady, pulling a heavy metal wrench out of his bag.

"I—I don't like it," stammered Foley. "Kill the weirdy kid? That's too much bad luck! We'll have to take him with us!"

Suddenly a police siren was heard in the Gore outside, followed by a rending crash from a side door and the bark of a German shepherd dog.

"Police! We've got no choice now," Brady said, advancing on Theo. "We'll never get away dragging him along. He's heard us talk, knows our faces . . ."

Brady swung the wrench back, ready to strike a fatal blow.

"No!" cried Theo. He raised a feeble hand in self-defense, grabbing at his attacker's wrist.

Then it happened.

Brady's arm stopped in mid-swing, as if frozen. His body glowed with a soft green light. And then, before their eyes, he melted.

# CHAPTER 3

# THE OPEN DOOR

IT HAD NOT BEEN A DREAM. Theo sat up in bed and saw the familiar shadows cast by the morning sun on the wall. He saw his bookcase of fairy tales and guides to manners. But when he closed his eyes he saw the robber, Brady, dissolving into a pool of oily slime and seeping into the deep hall carpet.

The events of the night before, brought to so sudden an end by the arrival of his guardian and the police, had left his mind scarred forever.

*My rare disease*, Theo thought. *My special condition, which, by the way — sorry we didn't mention it before — actually means that if you touch people they die.*

20

Theo shivered inside. He had melted someone. The killing had been in self-defense, of course, which Mr. Nicely had once told him was all right. But it didn't make Theo feel much better. Strange thoughts and doubts flitted through his mind, images he could not drive away. He recalled the picture he had seen of that hideous figure, the Dodo. How could a real man come to resemble an extinct bird? Suddenly his world was full of mysteries and misgivings.

Theo ran through the events that had happened after Brady had melted.

The old robber, Foley, had bolted—out through a side window—and hadn't been seen again. Dr. Saint had appeared and raced up the stairs without even checking to see if Mr. Nicely was still alive. *Not very saintly, Dr. Saint,* thought Theo. He didn't know what his guardian had done upstairs, but he certainly hadn't mentioned the secret room to the police. Theo didn't mention it either.

Clarice came in with a cup of hot water, Theo's morning treat. Tea was apparently too stimulating for him and might lead to enjoyment—never a good thing for someone like Theo. She proceeded to check his temperature, blood pressure, the circumference of his head, and the endless other measurements and readings that made his life a masterpiece of tedium.

"The thing is, Clarice," Theo said, "I was always told by Dr. Emmanuel Saint that I was a mystery baby—abandoned at one of the orphanages run by his Society of Good Works, with just a note saying my parents had died and could someone look after me."

Clarice searched for lice—or something—in Theo's hair.

"So what I want to know is," Theo continued, "why, hidden away in a secret room upstairs, is there a picture of a man who looks just like me?"

Theo put on a dressing gown.

"Secrets, Clarice. That's what you're good for. You can't hear, so you can't tell tales, I suppose. Is Dr. Saint being kind by employing a deaf maid, or is he actually being . . . careful?" Theo sipped his hot water thoughtfully. It was the only hot drink he would get all day.

"Dr. Saint has been keeping secrets from me, that's for sure," Theo resumed. "I can't help wondering about *everything* now. . . ."

Theo stopped. He was suddenly reminded of the mysterious gift he had received, the snow globe that covered a miniature London in black flakes. Had it been some kind of message? He needed to look at it again. . . .

"A special treat for you, Theobald!" came the strident voice of Dr. Saint from the doorway. Theo looked round. In came Mr. Nicely, his head wrapped in bandages, beaming a big smile—but his eyes looked rather glazed and he was moving stiffly.

"Your butler and—dare I say it—best friend is back on the case!" Mr. Nicely grinned. "I mean, back on duty," he corrected himself. "In fact, what I ought to have said is, 'I'm back doing what I love best,'" he added finally.

"You're rambling," snapped Dr. Saint. "Now, just a final couple of words about last night, if you can both bear it."

Theo looked around him. Here he was, in his room, back with the Three, the eternal trio that governed his life. But last night had been different. He had escaped the monotony—met new people. And killed one of them.

*It wasn't my fault*, he told himself. *I warned them about my gloves and they wouldn't listen. Terrible things happen to people who don't listen*—he had learned that from his books of fairy tales.

"Now, Theo—you told us you heard the intruders crashing around, but you stayed in your room the whole time."

Theo nodded. Yes, he had told Dr. Saint that.

"But you were awake from the first crash onwards, when they broke in and knocked out Mr. Nicely?"

"I tried to stop 'em, sir!" Nicely protested. "Four or five of them overpowered me!"

*More lies*, Theo noted.

"I was frightened," Theo said. "They bashed the door of my room in and had a quick look inside. They didn't spot me in the shadows. Suddenly the police turned up and they fled."

"So," summed up Dr. Saint, "when I found you standing in the doorway of your room, that was as far as you went all night. Of their criminal activities you actually *saw* nothing. But didn't you hear anything unusual?"

"Banging, crashing, footsteps on the stairs," Theo replied. At the mention of the stairs, he couldn't help giving his guardian a searching look. Dr. Saint seemed unsatisfied, troubled.

"Nothing that would explain a pool of revolting slime in the hallway?" Dr. Saint said. Theo shook his head. Just in time he remembered to show polite curiosity in other people's interests.

"It sounds fascinating — may I see it?" he asked.

"No," blurted out Mr. Nicely. "Horrible slime is not for you, Theobald Saint. Disgusting oily substances are not a suitable sight for the ward of the most respectable gentleman in London. Slime indeed!" Mr. Nicely tutted. He turned to his employer. "Possibly some homemade explosive cocktail that went wrong, sir—they may have been planning to blast their way into a vault or safe on the premises."

"We may never know," muttered Dr. Saint crossly. "But the Deep-Clean Team from Good-As-New Carpets have had a ghastly job shampooing it out."

"I've said a million times, sir," Mr. Nicely observed, "we should have security cameras all over this place and my mate Doogie from the old Horse Guards Regiment watching screens all day."

"Empire Hall is the seat of a charity, Mr. Nicely!" replied Dr. Saint, turning on his heel to leave the room. "Why on earth should we have to put up with oafish security guards and nosy television cameras?"

Their voices died away. Clarice gave a funny, bobbing curtsy and left too. Theo munched his morning bowl of seeds in thin milk. A long, empty day awaited him, while the Three went about their business. He would be left alone for hours. He went and found his mystery birthday present.

Theo opened the box, where the globe lay in its shredded paper like a glass egg in a nest. Who could it be from? He shook it and watched, as once again the black flakes swarmed inside. Had it really been meant as a message? Had the sender known that a shadow was about to pass over Theo's world? And if someone really cared about him, why hadn't they included a simple note or something?

Then it struck him. *The shredded paper*. Theo pulled the packing out of the box. He studied the strips closely by the light of the window. There it was—a glimmer of writing. The silver ink that had shown up so clearly on the black wrapping paper was barely visible at all on the white shreds.

Long years of confinement had made Theo adept at methodical tasks. He lay out all the strips of crumpled paper, silver-line-side-up, and started to piece them together. It was a fiddly business, but he had an idea. He prised open the framed photo of Mr. Nicely, slid out the glass and used it to flatten the strips under. It wasn't long before he had pieced together the words: *Theo. You are in danger and must get out! Come to the graveyard alone! —A Friend.*

---

"What are you doing, young master?" Mr. Nicely shouted from the hallway. He had found Theo standing by the study window that looked out on the back lawn.

"Just enjoying the view." Theo sighed. He hadn't been surprised to find the window was securely locked.

"You don't want to go opening them winders," chuckled Mr. Nicely, putting a firm hand on Theo's shoulder. "What have I told you since you was a nipper? Keep away from the winders and never set foot in the garden . . . there's something on the roof that wants to eat you!"

The butler hadn't wheeled out that old family legend for years. Maybe the bang on the head had shaken up the contents of his well-regimented brain a bit.

When evening fell, and Theo had eaten his millet and greens, he was left alone to study his books and listen to the quiet flow of the traffic as it ceaselessly circumnavigated Hyde Park. He had been in the Mercy Tube and was now feeling suitably sick. *That rotten feeling in your guts is us showing we care for you,* Dr. Saint had reminded him. Theo was no longer so sure.

He pulled back the curtain and looked out into the night. His own reflection stared back at him in the tall window pane. He looked at himself, considering his face in a new way. Up till now he had always been the invalid, the pathetic one, never someone who could be special or admired.

But now, when he looked at his tall, gaunt reflection, he didn't see himself. He saw the Candle Man.

There was a light tap at his door. Clarice was standing there, with a finger to her lips. She beckoned him. Theo was too surprised to act, but the maid grabbed him and pulled him into the corridor. She pointed down the hall, where two doors were open, one into the kitchen, and another beyond that into the garden. She pushed him towards the exit.

With his heart pounding, Theo blundered through a dark pantry and stumbled outside. The cold night air hit him, as he found himself on a gravel path. Clarice gestured to the rear garden wall, where a gate was standing open. It led to the back of the cemetery.

Theo was about to head down the garden when Mr. Nicely emerged from a side passage. His smart waistcoat was unbuttoned, and he was sipping some cider from a brown bottle and humming a little song. Theo turned, but Clarice had disappeared and shut the back door.

The butler hadn't seen Theo yet, but he was drawing nearer. There was no way Theo could cross the lawn without Mr. Nicely seeing him. Theo stepped into the shadows by the wall. Here he found a pile of crates. He climbed up on one, then on top of a big wheely bin, and from there onto the low pantry roof. With luck, Mr. Nicely would pass by beneath him without seeing him at all.

Theo held his breath. Then something flew down off the roof and carried him away.

CHAPTER 4

# THE SOCIETY OF UNRELENTING VIGILANCE

M R. NICELY STOPPED ON HIS way up the main staircase of Empire Hall and paused on the top landing. Something caught his eye, and he peered out of the window into the darkness beyond.

There, glimpsed through the cage of branches that cut off the mansion from the graveyard, was a tiny light. It had the frail but bright presence of a single candle flame.

Dr. Saint sat in his plum-colored dressing gown and took his mug of warm milk from the silver tray proffered by his butler. Mr. Nicely lingered at the doorway.

"Well, what is it?" snapped Dr. Saint.

"It's . . ." The butler's voice faltered. A strange light in the graveyard wasn't worth troubling his master over.

"It's what?"

"It's—err, ten o'clock and all's well," Mr. Nicely said. "I've done my rounds and locked up for the night. Not a burglar in sight."

"Just as it should be," said Dr. Saint, sipping his sherry. "Nice night, Mr. Nicely."

"Saintly dreams, Dr. Saint," said the butler, and headed off for bed.

———◆·◆·◆———

Theo was dropped over the cemetery wall and landed in a bank of wet nettles, his elbow cracking against a stone vase. A thumping of slow wings faded into the night air somewhere above him. He lay still in the cold and damp, his heart pounding, as the seconds passed.

*The Something on the Roof has decided not to eat me.*

Theo sat up and looked around. He saw a glowing candle on a tombstone in front of him. Suddenly a dark figure stepped in front of it.

"You're . . . you're *him*, aren't you!" the figure said. There was awe in his voice.

Theo was so bewildered, all he could do was nod.

"Did . . . did you see the garghoul that dropped

31

you here?" breathed the young man. From what Theo could tell, the stranger was barely older than he.

"No," said Theo. His terrifying flight had been something of a blur.

"We'd better move," the dark figure said. "Follow me!"

They raced down an avenue of yew trees, then threaded their way through a thick woodland, slanting gravestones marking every twist and turn of their way. Theo was led, at a speed he had never moved before, into the obscure depths of the Condemned Cemetery. Here the statues grew more outlandish, and giant mausoleums rose up among the trees. The starry, frosty night lent a half-enchanted, half-ghoulish light to the landscape.

"Don't worry," said the stranger as Theo paused to pant and overcome the urge to be sick. "Your captors won't really expect you to be here. Still, we don't want to take any chances."

They pressed on, along the narrowest of tracks, clutched at by thorny branches. Theo's elbow was smarting and his legs ached horribly. He had never been on a journey this long before in his life, even on his tenth birthday, when Mr. Nicely had taken him to see the city dump and they had briefly got lost among the mounds of seagull droppings.

They soon emerged into a clearing where Theo saw a small tumbledown cottage. It looked abandoned, with paint peeling off the door and one window boarded up, but Theo could see a dim lamp was glowing through the tatty kitchen curtains. In a narrow hallway, the stranger pulled off his coat and tugged off his woolly hat to reveal a mop of fair hair. His round red face and bright blue eyes glowed with excitement.

"Sam James," he said, "Society of Unrelenting Vigilance. It's an honor to meet you."

Before Theo could introduce himself properly, Sam pushed open a door and showed him into a small parlor. There, sinking into an armchair in the corner, was a shriveled, ancient man, so old his skin seemed to be almost transparent in places, with long looping veins showing through. His face was a crumpled patchwork of lines and liver spots, his eyes so pale they had no color at all.

*The cemetery keeper*, thought Theo. He looked around and, seeing no one else, was relieved to find that his rescuers numbered only two. The endless tyranny of the Three who had brought him up had made him come to distrust that number.

The cramped little place was a stark contrast to Empire Hall. This was a home such as Theo had read about in stories: a kettle on a small stove, a hairy throw draped over a shapeless sofa, a table littered with used cups and bowls. And a *television*. Theo eyed the forbidden apparatus warily.

"Welcome home, Theo," gasped the old man in an odd, gurgling voice that sounded like he was sucking in air rather than breathing it out. "I am Magnus James, Keeper of the Condemned Cemetery."

"Home?" Theo was starting to have a strange sinking feeling.

"Yes," said the old man, screwing up his tiny eyes, which made them leak some kind of gunge. "You will always be at home with the Society of Unrelenting Vigilance. It was we who left you that present—we who worked with Clarice. I won't shake your hand," the old man added, nodding towards Theo's gauntlets.

Theo's head was spinning. He wondered how much this ancient being knew about him. Suddenly he remembered how important it was to be polite to new acquaintances.

"I'm, err—delighted to meet you," Theo said awkwardly. "I hope you don't mind my asking, but what I really need to know, above all else, is . . . who am I?"

There was a moment of silence. Sam looked at

Magnus, as if hoping the cemetery keeper would say something. But the ancient figure seemed for a moment to be lost in a dream.

"They—they call me Theo Saint," Theo said. "But I know that can't be my real name."

"You're the special one," Sam said. "We've been watching you for years, making sure you're okay. And tonight, we actually rescued you!" Sam pulled a bottle out of a musty cupboard and poured a fizzy brown liquid into two glasses.

"And to think the garghoul helped us pull it off!" There was a strange note in Sam's voice that made Theo feel uncomfortable, but he couldn't quite place it.

"The garghoul?" gasped the cemetery keeper. He seemed surprised. "Well, well—the tide must be turning indeed!"

Theo was preoccupied by a *good-manners* problem. The two glasses on offer were so very different it was tricky to know which one it would be polite to take. In the end Theo took the elegant but tiny sherry glass, leaving Sam the huge but cracked wine goblet.

"This is what we've been waiting for, Grandad!" Sam grinned, swooping on the huge goblet. "At last our Society has done something! After all these years of just being vigilant, we've finally sprung into action and rescued the prisoner! This is the best day of our lives!"

Theo frowned. He didn't like being called the prisoner. Surely he had never been that? Magnus just stared into space, as if seeing faraway things instead of what was in front of him.

Sam started singing a strange, merry song. Theo sipped the liquid. It was disgusting. Theo now realized what it was about Sam that was disturbing him. It was the happy note in his voice, the odd sound of delight.

*Happiness, the most terrible thing,* Theo thought. The pursuit of happiness made people selfish and greedy — Dr. Saint had always made that clear. Now Theo was starting to feel upset. It was past his bedtime and he was exhausted. It had seemed to him that a truly wonderful person must have left him that enchanting parcel with the gold bow. There was no sign of that person here. He was sure neither Sam nor Magnus could have written his name in such beautiful writing.

"But who am I really?" he persisted.

"You honestly don't know?" Sam asked.

Theo shook his head. Magnus slowly raised a trembling, crooked finger.

"It is not a matter for *us* to speculate upon," said

Magnus in a lofty tone. "The Mysteries must be respected at all times. The Mysteries will light the way to the Ascendancy."

"What's the Ascendancy?" asked Theo.

"That's one of the Mysteries," said Sam. "I've never been let in on it myself." For a moment he glanced resentfully at his grandad, and it was clear to Theo who held the most arcane knowledge. Sam started pulling cans of food out of the smelly cupboard.

"We'll tell you what we can," Sam said, "after we've celebrated your escape."

---

Theo felt terrible. All he wanted to do was go to sleep, but in order to be polite he had eaten a huge helping of cheese on toast, smothered with mustard and piled high with baked beans. He had also drunk several glasses of the sickly sweet cider—to be a good guest—and he was sure he was going to die. His usual diet of millet and greens may have been boring, but at least it didn't make his stomach feel like it was about to explode.

"The Society of Unrelenting Vigilance is an order founded in eighteen ninety-two," said Magnus, sucking up milky broth from a bowl held in two trembling hands. "It is our job to watch over the Society of

Good Works and make sure they do not perform any—ahem . . . bad works."

Theo nodded to show he understood so far. He couldn't really imagine Dr. Saint and his charity organization doing anything bad, but since discovering the secret room he had the uncomfortable feeling that anything was possible.

"Anything else?" he asked hopefully. The cemetery keeper's mood suddenly changed. There was a strange glow in his eyes. For a moment, Theo was almost scared of him.

"It is also our job to preserve something special about the past," Magnus said. "Something which other people would try to destroy. You are part of that past."

"A dangerous part!" butted in Sam, hunting around under the sink for more cider. Theo went pale.

"Don't frighten him!" gurgled Magnus, almost choking on his milky glop. "*Dangerous* is a dangerous word. It is not for us to say!"

"But think how they locked him up, kept him hidden!" Sam shouted with his head still in the cupboard. "Theo must be very—"

"That's enough!" croaked Magnus, sitting up suddenly and letting his bowl crash to the floor. Sam shut up. Magnus smiled apologetically at Theo. The old man looked drained and frail again as he sank slowly back into his seat.

"This is a delicate matter." The cemetery keeper sighed. "Tomorrow Theo will be introduced to the Grand Council of the Vigilant. Until then, we must say no more."

Sam had failed to find more drink but appeared delighted to emerge from the cupboard with a packet of jelly beans.

"Anyway," he said with a grin, "you are so lucky we rescued you . . . whoever you are!"

Ordered into silence, Sam demonstrated his high spirits by throwing the beans up in the air and trying to catch them in his mouth.

<hr/>

That night, Theo slept on a lumpy sofa, with a smelly blanket wrapped round him.

They moved on before dawn. *My guardian must know I've gone by now,* Theo thought. There would be bedlam in Empire Hall! Theo couldn't bear to think about it. He still wasn't entirely sure he had made the right decision in running away. He shivered in the damp autumn twilight.

The three trudged through the scant woodlands at the edge of the great cemetery. Theo, still feeling a horrible gaseous reaction going on in his stomach, was grateful that the ancient Magnus was accompanying them, lurching along on two walking sticks. It kept the pace slow, and even Theo's feeble muscles started to get used to the activity.

They finally reached what Theo took to be the edge of the cemetery. An iron gate was snarled up in so much bindweed it took all Sam's strength to tear it open.

"I'm as excited as you are, Theo," Sam said as they squeezed through the gate. "I've never seen the Grand Council myself! The last time Grandad went, I think I was about three."

Magnus stopped and sank down between his walking sticks like a scarecrow that had lost half its stuffing.

"There has been nothing to meet for," he said. "The Society was created to wait and watch . . . until the time of the Ascendancy. That time is now."

"He didn't even tell me the rescue was on until seven o'clock last night—" began Sam sulkily.

"*Tush! Tish!* Keep it quiet," scolded Magnus. "The Mysteries must be respected!"

"All right!" groaned Sam. They hit an abandoned railway track, overgrown with head-high hogweed. The cemetery keeper took the lead and heaved his body along with silent resolution. From behind nearby dilapidated fences, the sound of traffic roared by unseen. Sam gave Theo a conspiratorial look.

"Grandad can't hear us now. He's hard to get away from. He's very, err . . ."

"Vigilant?" suggested Theo.

"Exactly. I can see he trusts you, though. He had that special look about him last night. He usually reserves that look for when he talks about Mr. Norrowmore."

"Who's he?"

"The Eternal Vigilance. He's the geezer we'll meet at the Watchtower. He's our only link to the Grand Council. I've been told it like a fairy tale by Grandad ever since I was a kid. Mr. Norrowmore sees it all. He points the way to the Council Hall. Do you know that stuff?"

Theo shook his head. "I don't know any stuff," he lied. He felt a bit awkward about not telling his new allies about the secret room and the Candle Man, but something held his tongue. There was something dreadful about it all. *Too much bad luck*, the old robber had said. And Theo, strangely, believed him. If Sam didn't know about it already, why should Theo drag him into it?

"You're special, that's plain," Sam said, almost crossly.

"I'll bet you know about the Eighty-eight as well!"

They turned a corner and Magnus loomed right in front of them, his pale eyes bulging with rage.

"I don't want to hear that number again, Samuel!" he rasped.

Sam gulped and nodded.

The three plodded on. Magnus took them through a gap in a boarded-up railway tunnel. Stumbling along the rubbish-strewn old track was exhausting for Theo and trickier still for old Magnus on his walking sticks. Halfway down the tunnel they turned into a side passage, up a flight of stairs, over a covered bridge, through something that looked like an abandoned ticket hall, and finally out into a weed-covered courtyard.

"The Watchtower," whispered Magnus, gesturing towards the dirty, decrepit old building before them. It wasn't a proper tower with a spire like in Theo's fairy-tale books. In fact it looked more like the tallest ruin in a collection of derelict railway buildings. Right at the top, a domed roof could be glimpsed among the broken chimneys and rusty aerials—one touch of elegance in the midst of decay.

Magnus produced a long iron key and turned the lock. "I signaled ahead to Mr. Norrowmore when you two were asleep last night," Magnus said. "He will be overjoyed to receive us!"

They reached the top of the staircase, and Magnus pushed a door open into a vast circular chamber. Theo looked around, wide-eyed. The top room was like a museum of communications. In the murky daylight that seeped through the narrow, barred windows, he could see robust old wireless sets, Morse-code apparatus, and enormous archaic computers topped with rows of electric valves. Vast rows of cubbyholes were stuffed with envelopes and packages, scrolls lay in plastic tubes, maps covered in string and pegs covered the walls.

But it wasn't the arcane paraphernalia that held the gaze of the three new arrivals. They were all staring at the skeleton in a suit that lay collapsed over the central radio set. Theo was the first to speak.

"I think we've found Mr. Norrowmore."

# CHAPTER 5

# THE SOCIETY OF GOOD WORKS

HIS MEETING OF THE SOCIETY of Good Works will come to order!" shrieked Dr. Saint. The room—which had been a ferment of panic, anger, and mutual blame—suddenly fell silent. Nine figures were gathered at the long table in the Empire Hall Assembly Room. Dr. Saint sat at the head of the table, with Mr. Nicely standing at the wall behind him, still with a bandaged head.

"To put an end to all unseemly rumor," Dr. Saint continued, resuming his usual outward calm, "last night, Theo Saint, my ward, was kidnapped."

There were gasps of horror around the table and murmurs of "I told you so."

"Details!" bellowed Baron Patience. "For pity's sake, we must move quickly, or our entire project is undone!" He mopped his bloodhound-like face with an immense hankie.

"Between the hours of ten o'clock last night and six this morning, the Vessel was abducted," Dr. Saint said solemnly. *The Vessel*—Mr. Nicely pulled a face. It was a long time since Theo had been called that.

"It was clearly part of a long-laid plan—"

"If you know it was long laid, then why on earth didn't you act to stop it?" Baron Patience asked.

"It only emerged that it had been long laid when my trusted housemaid, recruited from one of our own orphanages by Lady Blessing herself—"

"Don't drag me into it!" Lady Blessing protested, half hidden under an immense dark hood.

Dr. Saint ignored her. "It only emerged, as I say, when my house servant, Clarice Cripps, did not appear for work this morning at five thirty, as she is ordered to do. Mr. Nicely was then required to attend to my ward's medication and found him gone."

"Do we know who the perpetrators are?" asked a nervous, immaculately dressed gentleman in a white suit and lavender gloves. He was known in the Society as Lord Dove.

"Not with absolute certainty," Dr. Saint replied. "Clarice Cripps must have been part of a larger conspiracy."

"It is our darkest hour!" boomed Baron Patience, his enormous figure sprawled in a leather chair in the far corner. "If the Vessel should remain at large for too long, become independent—"

"Please!" cried out Dr. Saint indignantly. "Credit us with some intelligence! The Vessel *cannot* thrive outside of our protection. He has been brought up to be ignorant and weak."

A murmur of approval ran round the table.

"Theo was raised in splendid isolation," Dr. Saint explained proudly, "sheltered from all knowledge of the world, encouraged to mistrust the illusions of happiness and achievement. Even his diet was designed to . . . save him from the dangers of excess health and the follies of vigor. He will be unable to cope with freedom—"

"You assume he is still alive," growled the Baron. "If the Dodo has got hold of him—"

"The Dodo has been dead for over a hundred years," groaned Dr. Saint.

"Or the Taxidermist!" Lord Dove winced.

"One of our Mollycoddlers said she saw a garghoul on the wing last night!" said Lady Blessing.

"And to think I punished her for falling asleep and dreaming on duty."

Murmurs of dismay ran around the table. Dr. Saint waved his long fingers airily as if these speculations could be wafted away like unwanted smoke. The meeting was getting out of hand.

"We face no obstacle," he said, his face a mask of cold determination, "that cannot be overcome by our usual sworn methods of compassion and kindness!" There was a murmur of approval from the shadowy assembly.

"There is no alternative," said Dr. Saint. "We need eyes and ears everywhere—and hands to snatch our property back!" He paused for a moment, then spoke in a grave hush, pointing a pale finger towards the ground. "We must release our ancient allies!"

The company took a collective deep breath. There was a gasp from Lord Dove. "Not that awful *tribe*?" he asked.

"Yes, that perfectly awful tribe," said Dr. Saint.

"By Jove," rumbled Baron Patience, sitting back as if needing physical room to take on board this dramatic idea, "I like it!"

"*We* won't have to see them, will we?" whined Lady Blessing, her gaunt but beautiful profile glimpsed palely within her black hood.

"Leave them to me," Dr. Saint said. "I feel such remorse for allowing Theo to fall into enemy hands that I must atone in some way. Leave all the tricky details to Dr. Saint."

"A great, great man," mumbled Mr. Nicely in the background.

"What are we going to do about the police?" asked Lord Dove, fiddling with his perfect white cuffs. "You say they have actually been here—in Empire Hall? What do they know? What are they after?"

"It was an unrelated burglary . . . a small matter," Dr. Saint replied. Mr. Nicely caressed his bandaged head, which was not a small matter to him.

"Scotland Yard could be a nuisance," persisted Lord Dove, anxiously drumming his gloved fingers on the tabletop. "If they find out about the abduction, they will certainly want to know why we didn't report it to them!"

"They can never know!" snapped Dr. Saint.

"Inspector Finley is our main concern," Lady Blessing observed. "He has shown a little interest in the Society of Good Works before."

Dr. Saint folded his long white hands together in his habitual gesture of prayer. "A little interest is too much." He sighed. "Poor Inspector Finley has enough

48

worries on his head. I think an act of kindness is in order."

He pursed his lips in thought. "I have heard the inspector is so overweight, his colleagues fear he may suffer a heart attack one day. Perhaps if he were to win a contest—free cream cakes for a year?"

"I shall see to it," said Lord Dove with relish. "I am a lethal master of confectionery!"

"And he is partial to burgers and doughnuts. Perhaps if a cheap fast-food restaurant were to open right next to the police station?"

"No problem," said the Baron. "Our department of works will be notified at once."

"That won't be so easy," remarked Lady Blessing. "There's a children's hospital next to the police station currently."

"Get our friend the prime minister to close it down then," Dr. Saint snapped. "Goodness me, we send him enough friendly donations."

"It is rather a large hospital," Lady Blessing added.

"Excellent," said Dr. Saint. "I'm picturing a burger bar and two cake shops. After all, an honest police-man like Inspector Finley deserves nothing less. Work-related stress is a terrible thing, and I think this act of compassion will shorten his err . . .

*sufferings* considerably." Dr. Saint smiled as he received a ripple of applause.

"And certainly his life!" giggled Lord Dove.

"That is what I meant," said Dr. Saint, testily. "Now we must all be prepared. Our master plan, the Great Liberation, will go ahead as scheduled. Soon we will control dark forces beyond the imagining of ordinary men."

"It is what we have always dreamed of," rumbled Baron Patience. "When the sleeping army awakes, none will be able to stand in the way of our Good Works!"

Dr. Saint gazed kindly upon his fellow board members.

"We will see a happier world then," he simpered, almost shedding a tear. "A world where only the chosen few will suffer the worries of power and the burden of riches. A world where the ordinary man will enjoy the virtues of poverty, and the bliss of slavery. And, under our guidance, this nation will command a vast, docile Empire, as it once did!"

"Glorious," rumbled Baron Patience, thumping on the table and rattling everyone's china teacups. "Summon our disgusting allies then. Just give me time to get home and lock the door first."

Dr. Saint smiled, convinced he had carried the

day. "With them on the case," he assured the gathering, "I am confident that Theo will soon be back in our hands!"

———◦•✦•◦———

Six enormous men flanked Dr. Saint as he strode through the NO ENTRY signs at the gateway to the abandoned sewage-pumping station. The men, powerful brutes swamped in dark blue overalls, were known within the Society simply as the Foundlings—men with no family to miss them or ask questions if anything should happen to them.

"Who is that lump?" asked Dr. Saint, pointing at the dead body of a fat man in a Day-Glo orange coat, sprawled out on the floor.

"Maintenance man, sir," said one of the Foundlings. "Fence repairman or something. He spotted us breaking in. I had to—erm . . . relieve him of his earthly worries."

Dr. Saint frowned. "Well, make it look like he dropped his own mallet on his head," he said. "And get Lord Dove to find out tomorrow's lottery numbers."

"Lottery numbers, sir?" the Foundling looked baffled.

"We can slip a winning ticket into the pocket of our dead friend here," Dr. Saint said with relish.

"Then when they discover his body, his family will be too busy spending the lottery money to care about what really happened to him." The Foundling nodded and hurried away.

Mr. Nicely appeared, carrying a pair of brand-new Wellington boots. He appeared gloomy and distracted.

"Bearing up, Mr. Nicely?" asked Dr. Saint suddenly.

Mr. Nicely sighed. "I just had a funny feeling that I'd left something important behind," the butler said rather glumly. "Then I realized what it was — Master Theo."

Dr. Saint glared at him. "Pull yourself together!" he snapped. "Because if things ever start getting too much for you, just let me know, and I shall see to it you get a nice long rest!"

Mr. Nicely made a note to himself not to sigh anymore.

A huge iron door confronted them. It took two of the Foundlings, using all their might, to turn the wheel that opened it. Dr. Saint wrinkled his nose as foul air poured out of the doorway. He sat on a control panel while Mr. Nicely took off his employer's shoes and replaced them with the shining new boots.

"What on earth do you have in your nostrils, Mr. Nicely?" Dr. Saint asked.

The butler smiled sheepishly. "Lord Dove said it would be pretty smelly at the sewage station, sir," Mr. Nicely said. "The operations department issued me these nose filters."

His employer chuckled. "I hardly think an old soldier like you will need such a thing, Mr. Nicely," Dr. Saint said. "Pass them here." The butler handed them over in silence. Dr. Saint smartly put the filters in his own nostrils.

"I, however, am a more delicate flower," he said. "Now let us enter the network." The party trooped into the stinking tunnel.

"Pardon my asking," whispered Mr. Nicely. "But what are we doing here, sir?"

"Setting up that meeting with the old friends of the Society," Dr. Saint said, wrinkling his nose in disgust. "Not the class of person I would like to see a nice chap like you mixing with, Mr. Nicely." Mr. Nicely glowed. The old friendship was back.

"In that case, hardly suitable company for a saintly gentleman like yourself, Dr. Saint."

"Hardly," whispered Dr. Saint. "But back in the Victorian age, when the Philanthropist set up the Society of Good Works, he realized that there are two Londons. The glorious city of human endeavor we all know, and a second city—its shadow, as it were—existing alongside, darker, more dangerous. In order to achieve anything in the bright lights, one must also have influence in the darkness."

The soft wallowing of their wading echoed around them as they ventured deeper into the tunnel.

"Do you know where we are now, Mr. Nicely?" asked Dr. Saint.

"In the Monarch Fields Sewage-Pumping Station," said Mr. Nicely confidently. "I may be slow on the uptake, but I did manage to read the old notice on the gate."

"That is the sign we want the world to read." Dr. Saint smiled. They rounded a corner and were faced with a metal cage in a shaft, poised over a black pit.

Two of the Foundlings stayed in the access tunnel, while everyone else descended in the cage. It creaked and rocked as it plummeted downwards. Mr. Nicely flinched as ice cold drips ran down his neck.

"Invigorating!" he declared with false gusto.

"Back in the early days of our society," explained Dr. Saint, "the Philanthropist persuaded the government to let him set up a waste-disposal system down here, as a charitable gesture towards improving living conditions for the city."

"How typical of our revered founder," said the butler.

"It enabled the Society of Good Works to explore, develop, and exploit opportunities down here, in what we call the network. It provided us with unique resources . . ."

The cage had reached its destination. They stepped out, and softly glowing globes illuminated their way. Mr. Nicely had never seen these before, and peered inside to see luminous, living fungus inside the globes, providing the light. Dr. Saint led the party to a chamber, where banks of control panels rose up in the darkness.

"Our founder understood the subtle things in life," said Dr. Saint. "He knew that excess kindness can kill as surely as excess cruelty. He was also a master of alchemy. He knew that certain mixtures, when combined, could achieve quite magical effects."

Mr. Nicely smiled as all around, controls, lanterns, and bulbs lit up in a ghoulish mixture of greens.

"I am used to being in the company of genius," Mr. Nicely said. "So I shall strive not to be over-awed by these latest marvels, sir."

"We are going to perform a marvel, then depart at a swift pace," said Dr. Saint. He signaled to two of the Foundlings to step forward.

"Gentlemen," he said. "It is time to release the vapors!"

# HUNTED

THEO HAD NEVER SEEN A REAL SKELETON before. Until very recently he had only ever really met three people. Now he had encountered several—one of whom he had turned into slime and now this new one who was well and truly dead.

*Perhaps death goes on everywhere, all of the time,* Theo thought. *I just didn't notice it, being stuck in my room.*

Old Magnus had been very much moved. He stood next to the skeleton and spoke softly to it, as if it were still alive.

"You were a good man, Herbert," he croaked. "Vigilant till the end! You never abandoned your post, as you"—here he paused to gasp a bit as if his lungs were caving in—"as you vowed!" he finished with explosive emphasis. The old man straightened himself up with pride and stood like a soldier on parade next to his old comrade.

Sam suddenly slumped down onto his knees and buried his face in his hands.

"This is it! It's all over! Tell me it's not all over!"

"What do you mean, Sam?" Theo asked. Then he remembered they were not strictly on first-name terms according to *Acquaintances and their Associated Problems, Volume 3.* "Do you mind if I call you Sam?" he added awkwardly.

"What does it matter? What does anything matter?" Sam wailed from the floor. "It's over! Mr. Norrowmore was our only contact with the rest of our secret society! Now that he's dead, we're cut off! We've got no way of summoning the Council!"

Theo looked disapprovingly at Sam. Yesterday he had been all victorious, singing songs and flicking jelly beans up in the air. Suddenly today he was plunged into wretched misery. *Poor Sam*, thought Theo. Someone should have told him that merriment was a very dangerous thing to be messing with.

"Say something, Grandad—say there's a backup

plan!" Sam begged. The old man had now slumped into another of the radio-station chairs.

"Backup plans?" He smiled and tilted his mottled old head upwards as if seeking inspiration from the light filtering through cracks in the ceiling. "Plenty of those. Mr. Norrowmore knows them all!"

Sam buried his face in his hands again.

"Bang-bang, you're dead," a cheerful voice rang out across the room. A figure swamped in a huge navy greatcoat, with a black cap pulled down almost over her eyes, strode towards them through the banks of dusty monitors.

As she drew closer, Theo stared in amazement. It was Clarice.

"What—what are you doing here?" gurgled Magnus, his colorless eyes bulging with surprise. He clutched at Mr. Norrowmore for support, and the skeleton's arm fell off and clattered to the floor.

"Norrowmore ordered me to come. 'The day after the mission is done, go to the Watchtower,' he told me. He said that months ago," she added, glancing down at the remains of their leader.

Theo was still staring at her in openmouthed surprise. "Clarice! You can hear!" he blurted out.

"Of course I can hear," the girl replied. "But my name's not Clarice. I think we'd better get out of here," she added with a hint of nervousness.

"You *are* Clarice!" Theo protested. The girl shook her head.

"No time to explain now!" she said, looking all around the chamber.

"Why," began Sam anxiously, eyeing not-Clarice with suspicion. "Why did you just say, 'Bang-bang, you're dead'?"

The girl smiled. "Well, your tradecraft is rubbish," she said. "A Society member is found dead in a restricted-access room, surrounded by our secret files. You didn't even check to see if he was murdered. You stood right in the open, where any intruder could see you all—and pick you off if necessary. Pretty unforgivable, especially since you're with—you-know-who." She nodded at Theo.

Sam grew angry. "I can't believe you're having a go at us, with Mr. Norrowmore standing here, dead!" he said.

"Well, it's lucky we've got a cemetery keeper and a gravedigger on hand then, isn't it?" she remarked. Sam seemed hurt. Theo looked at the floor. He wasn't used to arguments. At Empire Hall people weren't generally allowed to have feelings about things.

"Listen, Sam," not-Clarice said. "We're at war

now. We've taken Theo away from that hideous Society and they will do anything to get him back. There is no room for—" She stopped speaking suddenly and put a finger to her lips.

"They're coming!" she whispered.

"Who's coming?" Theo asked. "Friends?"

"We haven't got any friends," said not-Clarice. Sam grimaced with dismay.

"What are we going to do?" he wailed.

"Get out of here! Run," ordered the girl. "Both of you—to the safest place you know!"

A fire-escape door was forced open on the far side of the chamber. An enormous figure in dark blue overalls crashed into the room, scattering a massive pile of old reel-to-reel tapes across the floor.

"They're here!" the intruder roared.

"Foundlings!" cried not-Clarice. She shoved over a tall bookcase, causing a chain reaction that sent shelves, piles of folders, and several decades of carefully stacked envelopes cascading across the floor.

"What are you doing?" gasped Sam.

Not-Clarice pushed over an old oil lamp, which smashed, spilling its contents onto the pile of papers. Then with great calm she stooped to ignite the pile with a tiny hand-lighter. In seconds, a terrifying blaze spread.

"Mr. Norrowmore!" wailed Magnus, seeing the skeleton engulfed in flames.

Not-Clarice propelled him and Sam to the door through which they had entered. "Go, now—run and don't look back!" she shouted.

"But the archive!" howled the old man, tears in his eyes. "All the Society's records!"

"That's the past. It's all about the future now," not-Clarice said. "Go!"

"What about Theo?" cried Sam.

"He's coming with me!" the girl replied, and kicked the door shut on Sam. There was an ominous roar as the fire reached the archive; row upon row of neatly filed papers went up like tinder. A giant man-shape blundered about, squealing, wreathed in flame. Two other figures appeared, lumbering through the smoke.

"This way!"

Theo was dragged by the arm towards a Victorian-style air-powered tube-messaging system. There was one tube for messages, and a larger one for packages. Not-Clarice bundled Theo into the package chute, and jumped in behind him. Theo plummeted into darkness.

"Where are we?" Theo's words echoed all around him as he followed the girl along a dark passage, somewhere far below the Watchtower.

"The network," she whispered, gesturing impatiently for him to keep his voice down.

"Are we safe?" Theo asked. "Are they coming?"

"How should I know?" snapped the girl, suddenly showing signs of strain. "You can use your ears, can't you?"

They trod the subterranean passage in silence. Occasionally a rat would scurry away from them. At intervals, glass globes of phosphorescent fungus provided a useful light.

"In the bad old days, the War for London was fought largely underground. The enemy had their rat-runs and we had ours. These tunnels are part of a vast system that's gradually falling into neglect. But I don't think those blundering idiots will have any way of guessing how we disappeared in the blaze," she added with a hint of pride.

It wasn't Clarice, Theo now knew. This girl, whose face and figure exactly resembled the housemaid's, was different in every other respect. She had a quicker smile, an angrier frown, and something elusive that unsettled him in a way he couldn't quite understand. He remembered some of the exciting characters from children's stories he had read and reread on endless winter evenings at Empire Hall. Not-Clarice had a quality he had never seen in real life before. She was . . . dashing.

*And I'm a useless invalid,* Theo couldn't help thinking. He was getting worried. It would soon be twenty-four hours since he had been in the Mercy Tube. He had never gone that long before without treatment. Oh, dear.

Theo suddenly remembered he had been told to use his ears, and he listened keenly for sounds of pursuit. It really seemed like they had escaped. They arrived at a kind of crossroads. To the left, an intriguing tunnel beckoned—a wide stairway of decorative stonework seemed to welcome him. To the right there was an underground canal, with a narrow ledge running alongside. A hideous stench arose from the canal, and thick vapors seethed above it, as if the whole waterway were a simmering cauldron.

"I don't like the look of this!" not-Clarice murmured.

"This way?" Theo asked, pointing to the first tunnel. His guide gave him a peculiar look.

"Nobody goes that way," she replied, striding towards the foul-smelling canal, "because of the Eighty-eight."

"Oh," Theo said blankly. He had noticed that once you were out in the real world, people constantly talked to you about things you knew nothing about.

"This is the safe way," not-Clarice whispered, pointing along the canal path. "At least it is usually. But there's something seriously wrong now. It's not normally full of this awful reek."

She wrinkled her nose at the foul-smelling vapor drifting across the surface of the canal.

"There's something odd happening down here. Still, we don't have much choice! Come on."

He stumbled after his guide along the edge of the underground canal. But almost immediately he collided with her.

"Trouble!" she whispered.

Emerging through the shadows ahead were two Foundlings. Their big bare heads gleamed like pale lamps in the glow of the fungus globes.

"Back!" not-Clarice said. But now they could hear footsteps from behind them as well. There was no way of avoiding their enemy.

"Trapped," said not-Clarice grimly. She turned to Theo. "Take off your gloves."

Theo felt a chill travel down his spine. What did she know about him?

"I want you to look very confident, stretch out

your hands and tell these fools to get out of our way."

Theo pulled off his gauntlets and shoved them deeply into his coat pockets. The Foundlings were almost upon him. He raised his hands, and in the weird light they seemed to be glowing. Did the girl see that too, or was he imagining it?

"What—what *is* this?" growled a worried voice from the tunnel ahead.

"Is it him?" a second voice asked.

"I don't know! You first!" the other urged.

Theo felt the girl push him from behind. He stumbled forwards, his long white fingers outstretched. The two men gaped in fear.

"Noooo!" the first Foundling screamed and staggered backwards, knocking the other man off balance. The two brutes grabbed at each other, tottering on the brink of the foul waters. Then, with desperate cries, both men plunged into the smoking depths.

"Reee-sult!" said not-Clarice, and she raced ahead into the darkness.

# CHAPTER 7

# NOT CLARICE

"WHAT DO YOU KNOW ABOUT the Candle Man?" asked Theo. He had collapsed, exhausted, into a silk-covered beanbag chair, in not-Clarice's attic room. After their escape from their pursuers in the network, she had swiftly headed back to the surface and taken him to a narrow but elegant old house in a tree-lined street not far from Buckingham Palace.

"Nothing," said not-Clarice, quickly. "Who's he? One of the fairy-tale stories Mr. Nicely is always reading you?"

There was a playful, mocking tone in her voice that Theo didn't quite know how to deal with.

"Why did you ask me to take my gloves off and run at those men?" Theo asked.

Not-Clarice drew back a lily-patterned curtain and frowned at the gloomy view of the gaunt mansions across the road. It was now a dismal afternoon, only two o'clock, but the dreary cityscape seemed to be already yearning for dusk. A faint mist softened the shapes of the stark winter trees.

"Well, they kept putting it about that you had a hideous disease. I thought we could make that work for us."

Theo fell silent.

"Hungry?" asked not-Clarice.

"Have you got millet and greens?" asked Theo hopefully.

"No," the girl replied. "I'll go and see what there is. You rest." She disappeared downstairs and Theo admired her exotic world. There was a painting of a beautiful woman in a long, fashionable gown. An ebony sculpture of a cat. A half-eaten box of dark chocolates. To Theo these things were every bit as strange as the skeleton in the Watchtower and the canals in the network.

Theo sank into his luxurious beanbag and gave a miserable sigh. Life had been awful at Empire Hall, but outside it was plain scary.

Not-Clarice came back up with a plate of blue cheese, crumbly biscuits, and pink cake. She had also made hot tea—which no sensible person would ever do. The dangers of that overstimulating brew had been made very clear to him at Empire Hall.

"If you don't say anything, then I'll be able to talk to you," Theo said, feeling a draft from the window and hugging his knees.

"You mean, pretend I'm Clarice," said not-Clarice.

Theo nodded shyly. "It's nice of you—I suppose—to rescue me," said Theo, breaking off a tiny corner of biscuit to nibble. "But things seem to have gone wrong. Magnus is too old and Sam is strange and disturbing to be with."

Not-Clarice laughed at this.

"We can't contact the Council," Theo continued, "so we can't find out who I am, or what to do next. That's pretty important, as I have a terrifying condition and I really shouldn't be running around free in the outside world. Soon, for the first time in my life, I will have gone twenty-four hours without being in the Mercy Tube. It's all looking a bit grim."

He took a deep breath. He was just making things worse. It was appalling manners to keep talking about *yourself*—the least important person in the world. He stuffed a pink cake in his mouth and swallowed greedily. "And now I'm with you," he added, "and the only thing I know about you is who you aren't."

The girl sighed and rose to switch on a lamp. Theo noticed that she dressed in fine materials; her dark dress and jacket seemed new and splendid, like things had always been at Empire Hall. Not-Clarice might be part of the secret society, but she clearly came from a different world than Sam and Magnus. Everything at the cemetery keeper's cottage had been chipped, tatty, old, or smelly. Certain things didn't quite seem to fit together to Theo, and he wanted a few answers.

"Are we safe here?" Theo asked.

"After the Watchtower turned out to be not so secret after all, I thought it best to avoid anywhere connected with the Society of Unrelenting Vigilance," she said. "In case we've been betrayed by someone. This is just a room a friend keeps for me. He's away," she added vaguely.

"If you're not Clarice, then who is?" asked Theo.

"Well, *Clarice* is," the girl replied. "She's my twin sister. I'm Chloe. We were separated when we were only toddlers—after our mother died. Clarice, who was born deaf, went into an orphanage and was chosen to serve the Society of Good Works. It was a great opportunity for the Unrelenting Vigilance. They adopted me and brought me up a fine lady." She grinned at this to show Theo she was making light of a longer story. "It meant they could swap me over with Clarice sometimes and get a look at their enemies."

"But why are the two societies enemies?" Theo butted in.

Chloe swigged the extremely dark tea.

"It all goes back to Victorian times. A very devious man, known as the Philanthropist, set up the Society of Good Works. This organization pretended to be a charity, but really it was just a front for a bunch of creepy villains. The Society taught orphans to steal, widows to be assassins, and sick beggars to pass illnesses on to their enemies. Even the police fell under their power. They had London in a grip of terror.

"In the end, some of the victims of the Society of Good Works — the people who had suffered at their hands — got together to form a secret alliance: the Society of Unrelenting Vigilance. Since then we've been watching — striving to stop this so-called charity from doing its evil work."

Theo's head was spinning. Had he really grown up in the heart of a sinister society? He felt anxious and miserable.

"I—I don't think Dr. Saint is just evil," Theo said very quietly, as if frightened of being heard and contradicted. "He—he's certainly a very clever man—with brilliant ideas." Theo stopped.

Chloe didn't reply. She was cheerfully brushing her hair, as if preparing to go out again.

"I suppose I haven't really known enough people to compare him with," Theo added sadly. Chloe gave Theo a sympathetic look.

"I tried to find out what makes him tick," she said. "Our Society took certain carefully chosen moments to swap me over with Clarice and get a peek inside Empire Hall."

Theo felt a tingle of enlightenment down his spine. He knew at last he was getting to some of the Mysteries.

"So sometimes *you* were looking after me!" he gasped.

"Once or twice," she said.

"What did you find out?"

"Not much," Chloe replied. "Even though they thought I was deaf, they never gave anything away. At Empire Hall they speak in a kind of code all the time. 'Looking after poor Theo' meant locking you away."

"Because of my illness," Theo said.

"Yes," mused Chloe, frowning deeply. She looked at Theo. "Do *you* think there's anything wrong with you? Or was it all just a trick, an excuse to hide you away?"

"I . . . I don't know," Theo said. His mind was

71

racing. If he touched people, they melted. Did that count as an illness? Could he really trust this strange girl, who wasn't Clarice, and her odd friends who had spirited him out of his old life and plunged him into a frightening new one?

"All right," Chloe sighed. "It's tricky. I admit this probably isn't looking like the greatest rescue ever. Magnus will find a way to contact me when he's safe. In the meantime, there's something positive we can do."

"What's that?"

"Find out if you really do have a disease — or if your guardians are just a bunch of liars."

There was a *beep* from the street outside.

"Here's our taxi," Chloe said.

---

Theo had been in a taxi before, with Mr. Nicely. It was one of the best things in the world. The London he usually only saw in picture books came dizzyingly to life as the cab navigated through the afternoon traffic. Glowing shops and bustling streets gave way to the hush and solemnity of wealthy mansions as they approached their destination.

"Why is Sam disturbing?" asked Chloe, smiling.

Theo gazed out of the window into an increasingly thick and nasty fog.

"He . . . he's one of those people who wants to be happy," said Theo.

"I see," said Chloe. "And that's wrong, because . . . ?"

"The pursuit of happiness makes people selfish," said Theo. "It causes friction in society and leads to a morbid fear of death."

"I see." Chloe wrapped a big cream-colored scarf round her face and Theo couldn't see if she was smiling or not.

"If people really enjoy life they won't ever want it to end," he added, remembering some lectures from his guardian.

"Wow, the Society of Good Works sure did its work on you," she muttered.

"And Sam throws jelly beans in the air and catches them in his mouth," added Theo.

"That *is* bad." Chloe sighed.

---

They were dropped off at the tall shining metal gates of a stately redbrick building in a quiet square off Harley Street. Chloe had to peer closely at a damp-speckled brass nameplate because the murky fog was getting thicker. She pressed a buzzer.

"It's just like that ghastly mist we found seeping out of the central canal in the network," said Chloe.

"Maybe it followed us up here," Theo remarked. For him, fantastical things were just as possible as real things; he had never been encouraged to distinguish between the two.

Soon, a distorted voice invited them to identify themselves.

"We have an appointment to see Sir Peregrine Arbogast," Chloe shouted into the security intercom. "It's Chloe Miles and Luke Anderson."

The electric gate swung slowly open. They crunched up the gravel drive of the enormous house. Thick evergreens towered overhead, dripping dirty fog.

"I'm giving you a pretend name," Chloe said. "Just in case."

"My name is pretend anyway," said Theo. "In case of what?"

"Think of it as a game."

A wrinkled, overly made-up secretary showed them through into a large marble waiting room, with an enormous stuffed owl on a plinth in the middle. There was a beautiful relief carved into the stone wall of Noah's Ark and the animals coming in two-by-two. Theo frowned.

"Funny," he remarked, gazing at the picture. "Most of the animals in that scene are the ones that never *made* it onto the ark—like the giant sloth and the unicorn."

Suddenly he grinned. "Oh, look, there's a sivatherium."

"Can we focus a bit here?" asked Chloe, who had never heard of a sivatherium. "We're going to meet the great Sir Peregrine Arbogast and he's going to examine you."

"Is he an Unrelenting Vigilance?" asked Theo.

"Shush!" urged Chloe, alarmed. "No, he isn't. And don't mention them again. Sir Peregrine is a respected expert on unusual conditions. I pulled a few strings to get him to meet you, as he's a sort of semi-retired recluse. Be careful what you say to him."

"Why do we have to see him?" Theo asked.

"Well, if you really have got a terrible disease, we need to know as soon as possible . . . so *I* can avoid catching it," Chloe said.

Theo's heart sank. Chloe was more worried about herself than him. She didn't seem to understand what a critical moment this was. Suppose this expert found out that Theo could kill people, and called the police to take him away? Suppose it turned out that everything Dr. Saint had said was right, and Theo had to go back into the Mercy Tube tonight?

"Luke Anderson," called a nurse's voice from down a dark corridor nearby.

Theo arose, feeling as if he had just been summoned for execution.

# CHAPTER 8

# PERSON THIRTEEN

"BOW DOWN BEFORE ME, YOU WRETCHED creature!" Dr. Saint stood by the Memorial in the center of the Empire Hall gardens and peered through the filthy smog at the small dark figure lurking on the edge of his sight.

The vapors had done their work. The forbidden substances locked in their rusting underground silos for over a hundred years had been released into the network's canal system, where they had combined, smoldered, and crawled to the surface to provide London with an experience it had not known for many long years: smog.

"I am not fit to bow before you," said the creature

in a sad voice, as it made a deep, if rather lopsided bow. "Only to serve you and be gone from your sight. Why have my people been released?"

"The Society of Good Works is preparing the day of Liberation," Dr. Saint said, "when all who were betrayed and forgotten shall be released into honorable service."

"Freed to be slaves!" cackled the figure suddenly. "It's like the good old days!"

"The lost, the pitiable, and the vile have ever been the concern of my caring society," remarked Dr. Saint. "And there are none more deserving to be reviled than the smoglodytes—denizens of the foul fog."

The child-sized figure grinned and stepped closer, not knowing whether it had been complimented or criticized. Through the murk Dr. Saint could see the smoglodyte's loathsome form. It had a bare, ugly head like a swollen fungus; a big, crooked gash of a mouth; slitlike eyes; and transparent skin through which a soft skeleton and pumping innards could be glimpsed. The creature lolled out its long tongue and tasted the toxic mist.

"A delicious air today!" it said. "But it comes at a price. What must my people do?"

"An act of great charity—seeking a poor, stolen

child and rescuing him from whoever has taken him."

Mr. Nicely appeared in the fog holding up a photograph of Theo's face and several items of clothing. Seen through the vapors they created the bizarre illusion of Theo's presence. The smoglodyte approached Theo's articles like a wary dog. Other shadowy faces appeared from the mist, gathered close, and reached up with eager fingers as if to absorb every detail of the articles.

"Act quickly!" ordered Dr. Saint. "Infest this city as you did of old. Pry into every corner until you find this person! Go now, you miserable vermin!"

The figures dissolved into the dirty air. Dr. Saint turned to Mr. Nicely, who was looking at his employer in a curious way.

"You have to know how to talk to these people," muttered Dr. Saint, brushing past him.

◦•◦••◦•◦

Theo and Chloe entered Sir Peregrine's old-fashioned consulting room. It was almost in darkness, with blinds covering the tall windows. The air was filled with a nasty odor, and Theo was surprised to realize there were dirty dinner plates and stained cups in little piles all over the room. On the windowsill was a row of dead plants, and fallen leaves lay curled along the top of the radiator.

Sir Peregrine Arbogast was a huge, saggy-faced man with scant hair on his head and heavy eyelids. He wore a thick gray three-piece suit with a broad waistcoat—from which one button was missing—and a greasy purple necktie. His face had an oily yellow complexion.

Chloe took off her big coat and hung it over the back of her chair. Underneath she was wearing a plain black dress and a string of pearls, which Theo thought made her look very respectable and almost glamorous. At least it made her look slightly less like someone who ran around sewer tunnels and burnt buildings down, which was probably important when arranging meetings with top doctors.

"Enchanted," said Sir Peregrine, nodding vaguely at Chloe. He didn't look enchanted, though; his eyes looked tired and dull. "I don't often take cases like this anymore, but since you obviously have such impressive connections . . ."

"All lies and illusion," Chloe said sweetly.

"Well, the best connections are," commented the old surgeon heavily. He flicked through a card index, then seemed to forget what he was doing it for.

*Person thirteen*, noted Theo. He had now met Dr.

Saint, Mr. Nicely, Clarice, Robber number one (Foley), Robber number two (dead), Sam, Magnus, Mr. Norrowmore (if skeletons counted), not-Clarice (Chloe), two Foundlings (possibly dead), a secretary, and now the doctor.

Thirteen was not an unlucky number to Theo. Because his life had been entirely dominated by three people in three rooms, he only hated the number three and anything, by association, that turned up in the three times table. Thirteen wasn't one of these contaminated numbers, so he felt strangely hopeful at meeting Sir Peregrine, person thirteen.

"Are—are you all right, Mr. Arbogast?" Chloe asked. The old doctor had been staring into space blankly but snapped out of it and looked at his visitors.

"I'm sorry," he sighed. "I haven't been sleeping well lately. Do you know," he added, scrabbling about in an ancient leather bag for some instruments, "when people cannot sleep, they begin to lose the faculty to separate fantasy from reality?"

"Perhaps there isn't any difference," Theo said.

Sir Peregrine stopped and looked up at the patient as if seeing him for the first time.

"Perhaps there isn't any difference," he repeated to himself as if to sound out the merit of the words.

"I'm sorry, you're catching me at a bad time," he added quickly, rubbing the white bristles on his chin. He stood up and stumbled on more cups and plates which had been stacked behind his desk.

"You should fire your cleaner," said Chloe cheekily.

"Never let them in here!" he rumbled. "Privacy is all important . . ." His voice trailed away and he stood staring into space again. There was another awkward silence.

"Perhaps we've offended you," said Theo. "I notice that Chloe didn't use the correct mode of address for a Knight of the Realm. I think that got us off to a bad start. Maybe we should leave." Theo stood up but Chloe forced him back down in his seat.

"Call me Sir Peregrine," the old man said, shoving the dirty plates aside with sudden energy and spilling spoons all over the carpet. "Now, let's begin properly." He pulled out a small lined card and poised an ink-stained fountain pen above it. "What was your name again?"

"My real name or my pretend name?" Theo asked.

"I'm sorry, Luke is slightly confused," said Chloe, smiling through gritted teeth as she kicked Theo in the ankle. "The fact is, Luke Anderson has been told for many years by an err . . . private doctor, that he has a rare skin condition. We want you to either confirm or deny that."

Sir Peregrine motioned for Theo to stand.

"Take off your shirt," he said, "and your gloves."

"Don't touch me!" Theo suddenly shouted.

Sir Peregrine stepped back.

"I mean, in case I'm . . . I'm contagious." Theo collected himself.

The doctor's face flushed an angry purple. "I have been in this profession for more years than I care to recount," he said. "And I believe I know how to conduct an examination! Now you take off your gloves and I will put on mine, and I will undertake to look at you without dropping dead on the spot!"

An unexpected sense of relief flooded through Theo as he held up his thin white arms to be studied. Unfortunately, the nearer Sir Peregrine got, the more obvious it became that the old man stank. The collar of his white shirt was frayed to a fine haze, as if it had been worn out decades ago. Silver stubble grew patchily on his heavy cheeks, looking as if it had been randomly hacked at by a disinterested party.

Theo stood like a pale reed awaiting a winter blast as the doctor inspected him from all angles.

"I suppose you think I'm a disgusting, decrepit,

foul-smelling old monster of a man," Sir Peregrine muttered.

Chloe smiled. "I'm told the best experts are often rather, um . . . unique people," she said.

The doctor shone a light in Theo's left eye.

"Head circumference twenty-four inches," interjected Theo helpfully.

"Why did you say," Sir Peregrine began, "that perhaps there is no difference between reality and fantasy?"

Theo frowned and ignored the fact that Chloe was making frantic faces at him and waving for him to shut up.

"Well, I've only been in the world a couple of days and it seems like everything that I believed was true actually isn't true, and some things I was told were just fairy tales, are actually—"

"Luke is a very unusual young man!" Chloe butted in.

Sir Peregrine straightened up. He replaced his instruments in his bag and took off his surgical gloves. He walked over to the blinds, touched a cord, and let a tiny glimmer of daylight into the room.

"I suppose," he said, vaguely addressing them both, "that when you woke up this morning, the fresh new day dazzled you with the infinite wonder of its possibilities?" There was a moment's silence.

"Of course," said Chloe, smiling.

"Well, when I woke up I saw this," Sir Peregrine said. He jerked the cord of the blinds and revealed a horrible gray fog pressing at the windows. "Murk. I've lived so long now that day and night seem to sort of blur together and become one thing. A perpetual dreary gloom that never goes away or leaves you a moment's peace."

He turned and pulled a pained grimace at them, which could have been an attempt at a smile.

"And I suppose," he continued, "that when you see people passing in the street, it would fill you with pleasure to meet them?"

"I would be glad to meet anybody," Theo said eagerly. "There have been thirteen so far if you count a skeleton and don't count—what does Sam call those flying things?" Theo asked Chloe, remembering the garghoul.

"Birds," snapped Chloe.

The doctor sighed. "It's a world of miracles when you're young," he observed. "But to me those people out there are a stream of rubbish. A pointless, annoying, spiritless tide of universal waste flowing through the sewer of existence. I've finished my examination."

The huge figure heaved himself back towards Theo and sat on the edge of his desk, his enormous backside bulging out in all directions.

"I'm glad you two came here today," he said, digging in a pile of papers for a big black notebook. He opened it and began writing. "I've been numb with boredom," he said. "Endlessly going through the motions of life. I thought I knew everything, had seen everything. But you are an unusual pair of youngsters. You've given me something I haven't had in a long while. A feeling of . . . surprise."

Chloe grinned.

"There's nothing wrong with you, Luke Anderson," the doctor said. "Nothing known to medical science anyway. Your rare skin condition is a figment—I would guess—of an oversensitive parent's imagination. What I am a little concerned about"—here he placed a hand on Theo's chest—"is a slightly underdeveloped chest, some muscle wastage, and signs of too little physical effort and fresh air, so I would—"

Sir Peregrine let out an ear-splitting cry and fell to the floor. Theo and Chloe leapt back as the great man's vast limbs thrashed about. Wracked with pain, the bulky figure rolled over and began to change.

His eyes sank into his head, dark circles of scaly skin forming around them. His nose protruded in a grotesque hooked lump. His skull seemed to shudder and throb, expanding into an ugly, immense dome. His clutching hands stiffened into hideous talons, while his body grew and twisted into a mis-shapen hulk.

As Theo backed towards the door, a shriveled gray claw pointed a crooked finger at him.

"It . . . it's *you*!" he gasped. "What a fool I've been! Why didn't I realize that it was you?"

CHAPTER 9

# THE UNEXTINCT

"Go! We've got to get out of here!" shouted
Theo, rushing for the door.

The grotesque shape of Sir Peregrine rolled itself
onto its side. A clawlike hand hammered down on a
red button built into the side of his desk. An alarm
bell shrilled throughout the enormous old building.

"Get them!" the doctor screamed into a large box-
shaped intercom. "Don't let them escape!"

Chloe clutched at Theo's shoulder as he darted
into the waiting room.

"What are we running for? We should help him!"

"He's—it's the Dodo!" blurted out Theo, tearing
himself from her grip.

Chloe raced after Theo as he headed back the way they had entered.

"The Dodo?" Chloe's mouth dropped and she clapped a hand to her head.

"Theo, what the heck do *you* know about the Dodo?" she shouted. Theo was now running through the reception area, not looking back. "Not that way!" shrieked Chloe, over the din of the alarm.

Two men in white coats had appeared in the hallway ahead of Theo and were blocking their way out. From his consulting room, they could hear the doctor roar, "Help me!"

"This way!" Chloe raced along a corridor that led towards the back of the house. Soon they were lost in a maze of featureless white corridors.

"There'll be a service entrance," she said. Rounding a corner, they saw a white figure up ahead, with its back to them.

"Down here," whispered Theo. They slipped through a side door that led to a flight of steps.

"This is bad strategy," hissed Chloe as they descended. "We'll end up trapped like rats."

Theo ignored her and just kept going. The stairwell went deeper than he had expected. Finally they ended up in a dank basement. Here the alarm bell was a distant sound, forgotten. Theo raced off down the first subterranean corridor he found, but Chloe easily caught up with him.

"What do you think you're doing?" she asked.

"If we keep going then we might find another way out—that they don't expect!" Theo said, making hopeful eyes at Chloe. She put her finger on her lips and they both waited in silence for sounds of pursuit. They could hear none—so far.

"They don't realize we headed down here," she whispered, "because any sensible people would have looked for the quickest, ground-level exit."

"Exactly!" replied Theo brightly. Chloe sighed and kept walking onwards. They soon arrived at two thick metal doors. Theo pushed on one and it opened easily. They were at the entrance of a vast, dimly lit chamber.

"All right, we'll try it your way, but remember—I'm in charge!" Chloe snapped, following him into the shadows. Then she stopped. She choked on the reeking air inside and pinched her nose.

"Wow!" she gasped. "This place stinks!"

"Even worse than the Dodo!" said Theo, treading cautiously ahead.

"I wish you'd stop saying that name," said Chloe. "Sir Peregrine Arbogast can't possibly—"

*Whack*. There was a sound ahead like someone

banging a stick on metal. They stopped. All they could hear was their own breathing.

*Cuk-aaaark!* They both jumped out of their skins as a weird, piercing cry shrilled through the air. It was followed by a muffled but heavy stomping that stopped as suddenly as it had begun.

They crept forward, their eyes getting adjusted to the eerie light provided by a blue electric strip in the ceiling far above. Rows and rows of elaborate enclosures loomed up on either side.

"Cages!" breathed Chloe. "What on earth . . . ?"

Theo stopped at the first one to look at a strange misshapen tree inside. Chloe came to join him. Theo peered through the bars and realized they were not looking at a mass of leaves but at feathers. The tree suddenly moved and waddled jerkily into the shadows of its pen, an enormous beaked head turned away from them.

"An elephant bird!" said Theo. "Mr. Nicely told me I'd never see one!"

Chloe gulped. "They're extinct," she said.

Holding their breaths, they arrived at the next cage. At first it appeared empty, but Theo drew Chloe's attention to a slumped, bony creature at the back of the pen. The moth-eaten, scraggy great cat was slumbering next to a pile of its own dung.

"Caspian tiger," said Theo, "figure seven, page three, *Woolcombe's Bestiary of Postdiluvian Extinctions*."

"Very appropriate. Because he's extinct too," said Chloe again.

Now Theo was picking up the pace. He beat Chloe to the next enclosure, an enormous walled pit. His eyes aglow, Theo gazed at the outlandish striped giraffe standing silently within.

"Sivatherium!" he whispered. "Look at those antlers! I'm glad he made it on the ark!"

"Okay, okay, I get it!" Chloe said. "Sir Peregrine is a descendant of the original criminal zoologist known by some as the Dodo—he's inherited this insane zoo of illegally hoarded rare animals—"

"Illegally?" Theo echoed. It had an odd sound coming from Chloe.

She ran up to the next pit and stared down at a serpentine head arising from an inky, stagnant pool. She looked back and forth as if committing everything to memory.

"Err, Chloe . . . what do you call those things with wings?" Theo asked.

Chloe stopped in her tracks. She walked over to join Theo, who had now reached the far end of the chamber.

"Do you mean the garghoul?" she asked.

"Well, there's a statue of one here," Theo replied.

Chloe rushed over and joined Theo at a thick concrete parapet that overlooked a bleak stone pit. Iron bars and a fine steel mesh partially blocked their view, but crouched in an alcove under the far wall was a gray, manlike figure, apparently made of stone. It had pointed horns curling up from its brow and a pair of batlike wings folded behind its back. Its eyes were lost in shadow. A large hooked nose dominated its face, with a glimpse of a thin-lipped, expressionless mouth. Chloe gulped again.

"You idiot!" she breathed to Theo. "This isn't a statue of a garghoul. It *is* a garghoul. It appears to be in its stone dream—a kind of trance they use, instead of sleep. Mr. Norrowmore told me about them."

She gazed in awed silence.

"I've never seen one before. I suppose I never really believed . . ." Her voice trailed away.

"Sam said one of them helped me in the escape," said Theo. "But I never saw anything. It all happened too fast."

"We have to get away and report this," Chloe said. "Lots of little things are adding up. Come on, let's find your mythical hidden exit! Maybe the garghoul slips out the back way to go shopping."

Theo smiled. That was more like the Chloe he

knew. But now they could hear the distant thunder of footsteps in the stairwell. Chloe pulled at Theo's coat and they explored the far wall of the chamber. Theo's heart sank. There was no doorway here, just a strange circular plaque set into the wall. Chloe stood frozen before it, as if she had seen a ghost.

In the corridor beyond the chamber, voices were echoing.

"Well, I say it *is* possible!" an angry voice shouted. "No one has yet seen them leave, so I say they could be down here!"

Theo joined Chloe to peer closely at the plaque. In the center of the circle, in jet on an ivory background was a weird representation of a black stream. "The sign of the River Styx! The way through the underworld," she said, her voice hushed with excitement. "This is the symbol the Society used to mark an entrance to the network!"

She knocked lightly on the symbol, *tip-tap-tip*, and a thin circle of light appeared in the wall. The fine line of brightness widened, and a perfectly circular section of wall withdrew slowly backwards, allowing them entrance to a secret passage beyond.

"It works!" Chloe grinned. "We're saved!"

As they vanished through the doorway, a stone head turned slowly and a pair of wings flickered with life.

CHAPTER 10

# LORD DOVE'S KINDNESS

MR. NICELY COLLAPSED TO HIS KNEES. He had tried not to scream at first, but after a while he had warmed to the idea. It gave him something to do rather than just wait for more pain.

*Remember, they aren't torturing you,* Dr. Saint had explained kindly. *They are simply doing their best with a rather experimental mind-reading machine. The agonizing pain is a by-product of Lord Dove's truth-seeking process.*

"I don't know where she is!" Mr. Nicely cried, his voice becoming hoarse.

Again the questions came, seeming to appear in the depths of his mind, and his brain felt like someone was pouring liquid fire into it.

94

"No—Clarice and I were never close! I didn't turn a blind eye to anything! I never wanted us to lose Theo!"

Just speaking that name took Mr. Nicely back to a better time. He had been happy then. He had enjoyed the pretense of everything being wonderful. He had realized at an early age, in one of the Society of Good Works' orphanages, that life couldn't really be nice, but you could pretend. And it was in the perfection of the pretense that you found your happiness.

With Theo around, it had been nice to have someone to look after, someone completely in your power. It had been fun to see the disappointment on his little face when his hopes and plans were crushed on a daily basis. Misery brought out a nice side in people, Dr. Saint was right about that.

"How could you not have known—not *smelled* that Clarice was a spy? The two of you worked side by side for years!" Lord Dove was screaming at him now.

And he had hit a nerve. There *had* been something about a smell. One day Clarice had surprised him by wearing a really chic perfume, the kind of scent a very elegant lady would wear—not a dull little maid. But he had only noticed the smell once, never again. That wasn't worth mentioning.

Mr. Nicely was in such a state of exhaustion and

distress now, he was flat out on the floor, his clothes soaked in sweat. His head was singing with pain from where those robbers had struck him two days ago, and it felt like it was about to explode.

He came back to his senses and found Lord Dove looking down on him, holding the headset and electric leads that had been attached to the butler moments before. Mr. Nicely gazed up at his tormentor with well-concealed loathing. The soft lavender-colored gloves, the white suits, the affectation of a monocle. Dr. Saint would never dress in such a vain fashion.

"That was most unpleasant!" Lord Dove complained. "You said you wouldn't scream. Not in the tradition of the regiment, indeed. You nearly popped my ears, you big baby."

The butler sat up. His head was spinning. For an instant he recalled Theo, staggering out of the Mercy Tube. Perhaps this was how Theo had felt too, every day of his life.

"You have Dr. Saint to thank for curtailing the process. He said you would have blabbered by now if you were hiding anything," Lord Dove said, turning away to accept a cup of chilled kiwi juice from Masters, his own servant.

Mr. Nicely rose to his feet and took a deep breath. He hadn't been hiding anything before, but he might do so one day—under the right circumstances.

Dr. Saint was in Theo's old room, which in the space of the last twenty-four hours had been turned into a laboratory. The Mercy Tube was now connected by several wires to a control panel the butler had never seen before, and all around there were computers and monitors. The master of Empire Hall had set up a work station in the middle of all this technological clutter.

"Where's my tea?" Dr. Saint asked abruptly, without looking up from a screen he was studying.

"I shall fetch it straightaway, sir," said Mr. Nicely, who had recovered enough to resume his duties. "The new girl, Veracity, didn't have the kettle on. She doesn't, you know, anticipate things like—like the other one did." The butler suddenly had a distinct feeling of having said the wrong thing.

"Oh, the *other* one anticipated things, all right!" replied Dr. Saint. "The coming Liberation, for instance, the fulfillment of my plans . . . And she tried to destroy everything you and I have worked for our whole lives," he added, bitterly. "So it is generous of you, Mr. Nicely—exceptionally generous—to have fond recollections of her tea-making ability!"

"Yes, sir." The butler turned to leave but his employer called him back.

"I suppose you're sulking because Lord Dove was kind enough to spare some of his time to eliminate you from suspicion, Mr. Nicely?" Dr. Saint peered at the butler over his reading glasses.

"Yes," said Mr. Nicely. "I mean no," he added. "I mean, whatever you mean, sir," he concluded brightly.

"Can't you see?" railed his employer. "We failed — abominably — in our task to protect the Vessel. We became complacent!" He got up, put an arm round Mr. Nicely, and turned the butler to face the window. Dr. Saint pointed out into the thick gray fog with a shaking finger.

"There is another Society out there! The Society of Unrelenting Vigilance! Doesn't that name chill your blood? For decades these fanatics have been watching us, spying on all our good works. But over the years, quietly, and with great care, we have been shutting down that organization, eroding its funds, discouraging its membership, even freeing some of its workers from their earthly worries." He gave Mr. Nicely a meaningful look.

"Killing them," said Mr. Nicely.

"With kindness!" insisted Dr. Saint. "But this broken, old, crumbling Society produced one final flicker of life. It actually managed to capture the Vessel."

Mr. Nicely grunted. He still didn't like that

expression. Dr. Saint beckoned his butler over to study the monitor he had linked to the Mercy Tube.

"But it's all here," Dr. Saint said excitedly. "In the Tube! Burned into its memory. Every day of the Vessel's life, every detail of the changes in his body. All the energy that was regulated, siphoned off, and studied!" Dr. Saint lowered his voice to a faint, excited tremble. "I think we may not actually need the Vessel anymore."

Dr. Saint flicked a switch and an outline of Theo's body appeared on the monitor, with waves of energy cascading through it. Mr. Nicely looked away.

"The Vessel is out there, now," Dr. Saint said, nodding towards the window. "Contaminated. If we don't repossess our property quickly, it—he—will become so poisoned by other people's thoughts that he may actually become dangerous to us. There might soon be a time when it will be better for the Society to free the Vessel from that contamination— from all his mortal worries, in fact—than to allow him to stay alive. When that time comes—will you be ready, Mr. Nicely?"

"I'll be ready, Dr. Saint," mumbled the butler quietly.

"Good man," his employer said. "Now let's see about that tea."

# CHAPTER 11

# FRAGMENTS

"HOW DO YOU FEEL NOW?" asked Chloe. Theo was leaning, red-faced and weak, on the gate at the back of the Condemned Cemetery.

"Sick, but better," panted Theo. The trip through the network had been as quick as only Chloe's expert knowledge could make it, but the air down there had been clogged with the dirty vapor that was now spreading throughout every nook and cranny of the city.

"What does it mean," Theo asked, "Sir Peregrine's having access to the network?" His face was resuming its usual pale hue; his dark hair was matted and curled by sweat and dirty fog.

"That your theory is right!" Chloe replied. "He *must* be the Dodo. But he was a weird villain from the Victorian days. How can he still be alive?" Chloe looked exasperated.

"I've no idea," Theo replied. "But I've seen an old picture of him—it's not the sort of thing you forget!"

"The trouble is," Chloe said, "Mr. Norrowmore always tried to keep me in the dark about the old days, the old characters. He wanted me to be *Modern Vigilance*—an up-to-date agent only interested in how to stop the Society of Good Works here and now." Chloe glanced back, anxious.

"Speaking of here and now," she added, "we'd better move on!" Chloe shoved open the rusty gate and plunged into the woods that surrounded the sprawling graveyard.

"Where are we going?" panted Theo.

"Can't you guess?" Chloe called back.

Theo hurried to keep her in sight through the gathering dusk. After a gloomy trek through the trees, Chloe stopped by a crumbling tomb carved to represent an immense sleeping lion. She motioned for Theo to remain there, while she scouted ahead. She scuttled through the smog, the holly, and the gravestones. Suddenly she straightened up, relaxed,

101

and beckoned Theo. "It's clear," she said.

***

The cemetery keeper's cottage had been trashed, taken apart by curious and destructive hands. Even items that couldn't possibly be important had been scattered and smashed, like the glasses Theo and Sam had so recently used in celebration.

"I should have known," said Chloe dismally. "There would have been a light on if they were here."

"What do you think it means?" Theo asked.

Chloe looked anxious. "That someone knew the Society of Unrelenting Vigilance had a house here. That they looked for clues. Then they wrecked the place to upset and frighten anyone who should return here."

"So you think Sam and Magnus weren't home when it happened?"

"I'm pretty sure of that. No signs of a proper struggle. This looks like an act of frustration, because they didn't find what they were hoping for."

"But how would they know where to come? This was all secret, wasn't it?"

"There are ways. Maybe they just followed a trail—your scent, I don't know."

Theo needed a rest. With his thick gauntlets, he brushed some glass off the sofa he had slept on only the night before, and sank into it gratefully.

"That's bad tradecraft," Chloe said, wagging a finger. "If Dr. Saint and his evil gang come back, they'll say, 'Oh look, someone's brushed the glass off here,' and they'll keep watching the cottage in case we come back!"

"Well, we won't be here," objected Theo. It still upset him to hear Chloe refer to his guardian as evil.

"No, but Magnus might," Chloe retorted. "He'll be trying to think of a way of finding *us* again. . . ." Chloe stood, chewing her lower lip and staring at nothing in particular. Theo could tell her mind was racing.

"I'm anxious," she admitted, "because it's really quite a bad thing that we haven't found Magnus here. It's also not good—and when I say not good, I mean very, very bad—that our enemies found this cottage, and the Watchtower."

Chloe pondered for a while. Eventually she sighed, tipped some glass off a wooden chair, and sat down too, looking glum.

"I've been doing all this by the book," she said at last, "following Vigilance orders. But now

103

Norrowmore is dead and Magnus isn't here. I think the rules have changed a bit."

Theo thought he heard a rustling outside, but he was too concentrated on Chloe to pay it any mind.

"What do you think happened to Sir Peregrine when he touched you?" Chloe asked suddenly.

*I have to trust her*, Theo told himself. *I would be a prisoner again if not for Chloe. I might even be dead.*

"You wrote it, didn't you?" he asked. "My name on the birthday present. The silver lettering?"

"Yes," said Chloe. "Mr. Norrowmore provided the snow globe. He knew it would intrigue you—enchant you—prepare you for our approach. It was a clue, if you needed one, to show you your life was under a dark shadow."

"It wasn't the shadow that intrigued me," said Theo. "It was the beautiful handwriting. Seeing my name like that was magical. It made me think that I—that life could be better."

"It can be," Chloe replied quietly. "It will be. But it's going to get worse first."

It was now or never, Theo thought. He had to tell Chloe about his power—warn her that he might be dangerous.

"I think Sir Peregrine was right," Theo began, "when he said that I didn't have a rare skin disease.

But I do have *something* inside me," he continued, his eyes lowered. "A kind of energy. It can affect people—make things happen."

Chloe nodded. "When we were in the network, the first time, and those Foundlings faced you—you glowed," Chloe said. "I swear you glowed, like a human candle."

"Like a candle man," Theo said quietly.

"Uh-huh," Chloe said, looking away from him.

"Chloe—I think you know more than you're telling me!" he blurted out. "How can you know about the Dodo but not know about the Candle Man?"

Chloe put a finger to her lips. "Let's keep our voices down," she said. "We should probably move on." But she didn't go anywhere.

"All right," she confessed. "I lied to you earlier when I said I didn't know anything."

"I knew it!"

"When I was a little girl, Mr. Norrowmore told me the myth one day. He said the Candle Man was a great hero. He had fought against the Society of Good Works in the olden days. It was a nice legend of good conquering evil."

"Except it's more than a legend. It was real," interrupted Theo, eagerly. "Dr. Saint has a secret room all about him. I saw a picture of him there—

and he looked just like me!" Theo stopped, looking faintly apologetic. "That's about all I know," he added.

"When I was older," Chloe said, "I was told never to mention the Candle Man. Apparently the enemy could bump you off just for knowing about him. That terrified me — so I buried the whole thing in my mind."

Theo was watching Chloe's face. For a moment there, talking about her past, in the gloomy, wrecked little parlor, he felt he had caught a glimpse of her as she was when she was a child — and he felt sorry for her.

"Recently, it came up again," Chloe continued. "I was working on the 'prisoner' mission. That was you, of course. When he sent me in to spy on Empire Hall, Mr. Norrowmore said it was possible that you were the modern-day descendant of the original Candle Man. I thought it was just a crazy dream he had. But after what's been happening — well, I'm prepared to believe anything."

"Why did you lie to me?"

Chloe scowled. "I was ordered not to discuss it with you. Norrowmore said it could only be done at a full Council — if we could get you there alive."

Theo gulped. It was terrible not knowing about the

Candle Man—yet dreadful to open up the subject.

"We need to know more about you—about him," Chloe said. "The enemy seems to have all the advantage—but there's one thing they don't have: you."

"Or you." Theo grinned. Despite the dire situation, he couldn't help feeling that with Chloe by his side they could do almost anything.

Suddenly he heard another rustle outside. Then a soft thump. He whirled around and saw a huge black rat on the windowsill—and it was staring straight at him.

# RATS

$\mathcal{T}$HEO SCREAMED. Chloe clutched at him.

"Don't scream, you idiot!" she hissed. "Stay calm. It's only a rat. It's only the biggest, scariest rat I have ever seen in my life."

The rat leapt down into the room, its sharp eyes gleaming with a disconcerting awareness. It stopped a few feet away, its pink nose sniffing up at them, its silver whiskers quivering crazily. The front door creaked and two more enormous rats the size of Jack Russell terriers squeezed through.

"*Three* of them!" Theo said, trying to hide behind Chloe. "Now that's got to be bad!"

Chloe stepped back nervously, splintering glass

with her heel. The three extraordinary creatures began to circle them silently.

"What kind of rats are they?" Chloe wondered, horrified.

"Siberian wolf rats," Theo said. "Page seventy-two, *Woolcombe's Bestiary of Postdiluvian Extinctions*. And — as *you* would say — extinct."

The rodents suddenly stopped circling, sat back on their haunches, and threw back their heads, showing long white teeth. Then they let out a queer, high-pitched whine that grew louder and louder, turning into a hideous ear-splitting squeal.

"We've just been identified and pinpointed," Chloe said. "I'm betting the Dodo won't be far behind. We've got to get away fast!" She bundled Theo ahead of her, straight out of the door, with the rats in close pursuit.

Chloe paused in the little clearing, glancing around for their best exit. Through the dusky woods, they could see four men in goggles and white coats running towards them — the Dodo's men.

"Of course — they came down the network behind us!" groaned Chloe. "Any bright ideas?"

Then the shadows fell. From out of the trees they dropped, child-sized silhouettes descending on the white-coated men and pulling them to the ground.

Theo and Chloe gazed, horrified, as the Dodo's men struggled and sank under the attack of the nightmarish forms. Suddenly, from a nearby thicket, a single shadow sprang towards Theo and Chloe.

There it stood, an ugly, gloating imp, with a face like a crudely cut jack-o'-lantern. Its skin was stretched over its soft bones like a plastic bag, revealing bubbling gas and shriveled organs pulsating inside. A long gray tongue was hanging out, and a pale light burnt in its eyes.

"Smoglodytes!" gasped Chloe.

"He is ours!" screeched the creature. It bounded towards Theo but was pounced on by the three rats. A horrible cry pierced the air as the ferocious rodents attempted to rip the airy bag of the smoglodyte's body to pieces. Chloe didn't have to tell Theo to run.

The hunted pair fled through the woods, squeals and whimpers fading in the dirty air behind them. No longer caring if they were seen, they headed straight for one of the main pathways. A bent old woman placing roses on a grave turned and looked in surprise to see two figures tearing helter-skelter through the tombs.

Amazed at their own progress, they stumbled out into the dazzling electric light of a busy city street, and grinned at the enormous friendly form of a big red double-decker bus.

* · ✦ · *

"Wake up," said Chloe, shaking Theo by the shoulder. He had fallen asleep on the leather sofa in the tall old house they had been in earlier that day. Chloe gave Theo a drink of hot water. He cupped his hands around the big green china mug and peered down through the steam at his blistered bare feet. He wiggled his sore toes. He wasn't used to any kind of exertion, and it was only now that he fully realized the damage his delicate body had sustained.

It was hard to believe he was back, safe in Chloe's mysterious world of luxury after all their adventures.

"Not much food left, I'm afraid," she said, sitting next to him. "Smoked salmon on crispbread. Tinned artichoke hearts for dessert." The squeak of some brakes in the street made Theo jump, but Chloe shook her head.

"We would've been tracked down by now if the Dodo's unearthly menagerie was still on our scent. I'm guessing the two different groups of attackers pretty much slaughtered each other."

"That would be great," Theo said.

Chloe frowned.

"When you get older," she chided, "you'll come to regard any loss of life as a pity."

"Not gigantic rats," said Theo. "I kind of liked the smoglodyte, though," he added. "He isn't in any of my books. Mr. Nicely must have been saving him up."

"Oh, Mr. Nicely has been saving him up, all right," said Chloe. "The smogs were imprisoned over a hundred years ago. Magnus told me about them once. Apparently they were used as spies on the street in Victorian times. They can only survive in filthy smog. Now it looks like the Society of Good Works has brought them—and the smog—back again to track you down."

Theo peeled away a slimy morsel of smoked fish, put it back on the plate, and bit into some crispbread. He was pleased to find it had a plain, wholesome drabness to it. He was only used to boring food and wanted the comfort of it now.

"Have *we* got any plans?" Theo asked.

"Mr. Norrowmore had all the ideas, and the fall-backs." Chloe sighed. "A man obsessed with secrecy unexpectedly dies, leaving his secret society in bits with no notion of what to do next." For once her face looked drawn and tired.

"There must be something! I thought you were a

big organization — Great Council of the Vigilant and so on. Lighting the way to the Ascendancy."

"Do you know about the Ascendancy?" asked Chloe eagerly.

"No. Only that Magnus said the time for it was right now."

Chloe looked troubled. She drained her black tea, ignoring Theo's disgusted look.

"I only wish there *were* a Council to help us," she said. "We were a big group once. But the Society of Good Works has been shutting us down. There were two old brothers, the Howes. The Know-Howes, we used to call them. Experts on the garghouls, smoglodytes, things like that. They were murdered two years ago by Foundlings. Then there was an old scientist, Mr. Arklow — he's vanished without a trace. Maybe Mr. Norrowmore was killed too, in the Watchtower. We'll probably never know."

"Not now that you've torched the place and destroyed all the evidence," Theo remarked.

"Exactly," Chloe replied. "Another one of my brilliant ideas. Like taking you to have a checkup with the Dodo. I've been on a roll since this crisis kicked off."

Theo grinned. "You've been unrelentingly vigilant," he reassured her. "You haven't let me out of your sight."

Chloe looked pleased. "We need to act," she decided. "Since we're working alone and have the hounds of hell after us—"

Theo went pale.

"Not the actual hounds of hell," Chloe groaned. "Since we're in a tricky spot, we have to follow up our one advantage. What scares them most is you. We need to find out the truth behind this Candle Man business."

Theo sipped his hot water and pondered.

"There is someone else," he said. Theo paused, unsure whether or not to go on. *This is it,* he thought. *I'm heading straight into the terrible thing. The ancient myth that makes grown men turn white and run away.*

"Go on," said Chloe gently, fishing a dripping artichoke heart out of a tin.

"An old burglar. He knows things. His name's Foley. If we could find him he might . . ." Theo's voice trailed off miserably. "I'm joking. How are two people like me and you going to find one old robber in an enormous city like this?"

"We might," said Chloe, reaching for the telephone. "Because there's something I haven't told you."

Theo looked up at her, intrigued.

"I'm also connected to another very secretive society," Chloe said. "We're called the police."

# CHAPTER 13

# ON THE CASE

"TAKE THAT MISERABLE look off your face," said Chloe.

Theo sank down in the threadbare armchair at the back of the coffeehouse and glowered at the world around him. They were in a gloomy dive near Clapham Common. Chloe had brought them here in a taxi from St. James's Park, and Theo had sat agog at the sheer size of the city around him.

"Just relax." Chloe smiled, throwing her big navy greatcoat onto a sofa with her bag. "Things are looking up. Wait here and I'll get you a coffee."

"Are you stark raving mad?" Theo blurted out.

"Just get me some water. Oh, and see if they've got pink cake."

"I get it, coffee is bad for you, and so is smiling and so is trusting people."

"The police aren't just people," Theo said. "I know all about them. They've invented this thing called the Law. It can decide who is good and bad, and—get this—it can put you in a prison."

"Well, you're used to that," Chloe replied, heading off.

*She isn't the Chloe I thought she was*, Theo said to himself. *She's tricky.* He peered around. A young couple in fashionable clothes were laughing and joking at a table by the window. Theo scowled.

"Seen someone you know?" teased Chloe, returning with a heavily laden tray. "Aha, here's Mike now!"

A tall, skinny man with narrow eyes and a tiny moustache stepped into the café, looking around nervously. He seemed older than Chloe but younger than Dr. Saint. He wore a lumpy brown suede jacket and super-shiny shoes. Theo smiled at the ugly jacket, but there was a hint of Empire Hall about those shoes. Theo realized now that posh clothes depressed him.

"Who's this?" the man asked, diving into an armchair next to Chloe.

"Luke Anderson," Chloe said.

116

"Your friend who had the stuff nicked?"

"Yes. Luke, this is Mike"—Chloe lowered her voice to a whisper—"*Sergeant* Crane." The policeman went to shake hands but saw that Theo was sitting on his. Theo wasn't surprised to see that Crane readily accepted a large coffee nudged towards him by Chloe. *The Brown Death*, Theo noted to himself.

"Well, I've found Foley for you," Crane said. "Male, Caucasian, seventy-two. Professional safe-cracker and housebreaker, semi-retired, especially since they brought all that new technology in. Three stretches inside. No assault, nothing hard-core. He's just a pathetic weasel. Now a pathetic *old* weasel. Had a younger partner, last we heard. Brady. Now *he*'s got serious form. Thirtysomething, shaven head. Don't go anywhere near him."

*We won't*, thought Theo.

"So where can we find Foley?" Chloe asked.

"Can we speak in front of him?" the sergeant asked, glancing at Theo.

"Yes," said Chloe. "Luke knows everything."

"Everything?"

"Ask him about postdiluvian extinctions," suggested Chloe.

Crane pulled a face. "What are you up to, Chloe?" he asked.

"Ongoing investigation, sir," she said.

"Investigation into how to bleed my department of funds for two years and produce nothing in return," Crane said, glancing around the room.

"It's called deep cover," Chloe said, a little frown knitting fine lines in her brow. "I'm being accepted, getting to know all these secret societies, before we assemble our case. I wouldn't be meeting you if it wasn't for all this smog and the fact that you insisted."

Theo frowned. Was Chloe telling the truth? Had she really become involved with the Society of Unrelenting Vigilance simply to get evidence for her police case? Or was she just telling Crane that to keep him happy? Chloe's fondness for weaving tales made his head spin. Is this what people in the outside world did all the time? No wonder he was always getting confused about what was real and what wasn't.

"I have to tell the boss I've actually seen you," Crane was saying uncomfortably.

"How is our boss? I miss him," Chloe commented.

"Oh, Finley, he's never been happier. Just won some cream-cake competition, lucky so-and-so. Face never out of a bun."

"Delightful," Chloe groaned.

"It's like this, Chlo'," Crane said, draining his cup.

"I'm going to need some results soon, or the department will just kill the whole case." Crane sounded more anxious than angry.

"Give me Foley then," Chloe said.

---

Theo held his breath as he heard the slow footsteps clomp up the stairs. It had been a simple matter for Chloe to force the cheap lock of this dingy, one-room flat, and now they waited in the darkness for their quarry to arrive.

The door was shoved open and the old man entered. Flicking a switch on the wall, the man cursed when the light failed to come on. Muttering, he felt his way towards the kitchen area and bent down to rummage around for a spare bulb under the sink.

"Police!" Chloe shouted.

"Ow!" The man leapt up, cracked his head on a hanging saucepan, and staggered forwards into the room. He tripped over a coffee table and landed in a heap on the carpet.

Theo and Chloe were sitting side by side on the sofa. The streetlights outside the tatty curtains threw just enough light to cloak them both in shadow. That was how Chloe had planned it.

"Special Detective Cripps," she said, using a lighter to reveal a glimpse of her identity card. "We just want to ask you a couple of questions, Mr. Foley."

Foley pushed himself up from the floor and sat kneeling, still rubbing his head.

"How did you get in here? Why all the cloak-and-dagger stuff?" he asked, trying to sound defiant.

"Door was open, light's on the blink," said Chloe. Theo could see her fingering the bulb she pushed deep into her coat pocket. "Didn't think you'd mind." She had wanted to catch the old villain at maximum disadvantage, and she clearly had.

Foley stood up shakily.

"I'm not answering nothing. It's all highly irregular!" he moaned.

"Cooperate with us," Chloe said, "and we might be lenient over the Empire Hall job."

"Em — Empire Hall?" stammered the old man. He was blustering but sounded ready to crack. "That wasn't me! Now you get out of here!"

"I was there, Mr. Foley," said Theo quietly.

There was a moment of stunned silence. Chloe calmly held her lighter under Theo's face so Foley could recognize him by the single yellow flame.

"It — it's Weirdy!" Foley gasped, and fell back to his knees. "Don't — don't let him near me!"

Chloe glanced at Theo. "You obviously made a big impression."

"It's—err . . . nice to see you again," said Theo politely.

"Have you come for me?" Foley asked Theo in a shaking voice. "Is it my—my time?" he quavered.

"It *will* be your time if you don't pull yourself together," Chloe snapped, helping Foley into a chair. "Now all we want is some answers." The haggard figure looked up at Theo with imploring eyes.

"I knew you'd find me," the terrified man said. "The legend says there's no escape. I've pretty much just sat here waiting for you. You're not going to do that thing to me, are you?" he sobbed.

Chloe looked at Theo with new respect. Somehow he had inspired dread in this cynical old villain.

"I want you to tell me what you know about the Candle Man," said Theo.

# CHAPTER 14

# OUT OF PRINT

"Some sort of ritual, is it?" the old man said, grimacing. "My last confession — as it were?"

"Maybe," said Chloe, darkly. The darkness hid the burglar's pimpled skin and broken teeth, erasing the years and giving a glimpse of a more vigorous man.

"First heard about him when I was a lad," began Foley.

"Is this the long version?" interrupted Chloe rudely. "We haven't got all night!"

Theo elbowed her.

"I knew about it from my grandad," Foley carried on. "He owned the shop below here, the engraving business. He loved pictures. Especially horrible ones. Like the scenes of murders they used to run in the old picture papers." An ugly relish lit up Foley's face.

Theo held his breath and let the burglar ramble on. He didn't mind the long version.

*We're going back into the secret room*, Theo thought, his mind picturing the hidden study in Empire Hall, filled with the forbidden things. He knew that what he was about to hear would affect his whole destiny.

"Anyway, he liked grisly stories too. He especially liked the old Victorian stuff. *Hound of the Baskervilles*, that kind of thing. But Grandad had his special favorite. True-life murder mysteries. Based on the exploits of Lord Wickland, scourge of the under-world. The legend went that Wickland's body would glow if he was in the presence of a murderer. That started up his name—Candle Man. But there was another side to it—more awful . . ." The old man began nibbling nervously at his bottom lip.

Theo held his breath. He could guess what was coming. He knew only too well that there was more to the power than just glowing in the dark. But now at least he had a name to conjure with—an intriguing name: *Lord Wickland.*

"Anyway, some of the stories was like that," Foley continued. "Wickland takes on the underworld. But others were more far-fetched. The Candle Man had enemies—the Dreadful Dodo and the Terrible Taxidermist. Dr. Pyre was another one—the Incinerated Man, they called him. I think my favorite book was *Slaughter of the Gargoyles*—now, that was a creepy one."

Theo and Chloe exchanged a glance, remembering the garghoul imprisoned under the Dodo's house.

"Grandad had the complete set. Then we heard someone was collecting them all, buying them up. They quickly vanished off all the bookshelves. You never even saw them in rummage sales. The publisher suddenly went out of business. It was funny—one minute Candle Man was as popular as Sherlock Holmes, the next, not a trace.

"Well, some people in the trade knew about Grandad's collection. A posh bloke came round to see us one day. Pulled out a roll of notes in front of us all, and offered to buy the whole lot. Grandad was happy. 'I'm sitting on a gold mine,' he says. I was pleased, 'cause we never had much money. Hoped he might buy me some lead soldiers.

"But Grandad wouldn't sell. He said the Wickland stuff had got so rare the price could only go up and up. The posh bloke was furious. Told us he was from some kind of important charity. Was Grandad going to stand in the way of vital charity work? Well, Grandad told him to get lost.

"About a month later we had a funny letter from the government. Department of Toxicology or something. It said all picture magazines from a certain period had accidentally been printed with toxic ink. Dangerously poisonous. It said men would be calling around to check.

"Well, just a day later, these blokes forced their way in: couple of brutes and a posh geezer in a hat and scarf lurking behind them, directing operations.

"Grandad was furious. 'It's you, isn't it?' he said to the posh geezer looking through all his stuff. 'You're that bloke who was here before!' Then one of the brutes knocked Grandad to the floor. I didn't understand it. I was only a nipper and I burst into tears. They found his precious collection and took it away.

"'You're just after my Candle Man books!' Grandad shouts. This made the posh gent come back for a moment. 'That name is unlucky,' he says. 'Breathe it again, and it'll be your last.'

"Grandad died not long after. Poison from them old magazines, a doctor came and told us. Said

Grandad should have given them up years before."
Foley fell silent. Time seemed to slow down as Theo
waited for the old man to continue. Suddenly Foley
leant forwards, becoming more conspiratorial.

"Before Grandad died, he told me the whole truth.
One evening he was sitting up in bed as if he was
going to get better. He called me in, just for a chat.
But when I shut the door he looked all serious. Said
there were important things that had to be remembered. He said the reason he had hung on to them
Candle Man stories was because they were part of
his life — they were all true!

"Grandad said he had been in one of the gangs
when he was younger. He had guarded some prisoner, run some guns, delivered some livestock for
the Dodo. That's right — all them grisly characters
was *real*."

"Wait!" Chloe stepped lightly to the window and
twitched the curtain back. There was nothing outside but the fog and the glare of traffic crawling by
in the street.

*Don't stop him now*, thought Theo. With every word
he could feel his destiny drawing closer. He had
always guessed, throughout his long, dreary childhood at Empire Hall, that life in the outside world
could never be as dull and matter-of-fact as his

guardians had led him to believe. Foley was right—the things that people said were just stories could all turn out to be true.

Chloe turned away from the window, frowning. "Ignore me," she muttered. "I'm getting paranoid."

"I didn't hear nothing," Foley said. "We're two floors up anyway."

"I know," said Chloe quietly. "Go on."

Theo noticed that Chloe had stopped baiting the old man. It seemed Foley had been touched by the bad luck too. His grandad had obviously been robbed of his Candle Man books by the Society of Good Works, then killed to keep him quiet. As Foley continued his tale, Theo began to feel they were no longer speaking as enemies. They were falling under the same shadow—all in it together.

"In those days there were more blokes around who knew this stuff," said Foley, "men who had been through the *war*, met the bigwigs. My grandad had it confirmed from one or two lads who had seen it firsthand. They all lived in terror of Lord Wickland. His name alone was worth more than a hundred men to the police. He wasn't just called the Candle Man because his body would glow in the presence of a murderer. He had a *death touch*. He only had to put his hand on an enemy and their skin and bones—

even the clothes they were wearing—would bubble up and melt away. There was this saying: 'Evil melts like wax at the hands of the Candle Man.'"

Foley stared up at Theo, ghostly white. "I only ever half-believed it until, until . . ."

"Until what?" pressed Chloe.

"Until I met *him*." Foley gulped, shrinking away from Theo so much he nearly fell off his chair.

Theo could feel Chloe's curious gaze burn into him. She must know now that he had used his deadly powers. He didn't mind. He looked at his own hands in awe. He gazed down at the old robber, a hardened villain, who cringed at Theo's mere presence. He experienced a strange, not unpleasant sensation—one he had scarcely known before in his life—a feeling of power.

*I am not Theo Saint*, he told himself. *I am Theo Wickland. Last descendant of the original Candle Man.*

"Look," Chloe butted in, "do you want to help get revenge on the people—the so-called charity—who helped to murder your grandad? We can help you. But only if you tell us everything you know."

"Already have," sighed Foley. "Never witnessed none of it myself. Just heard the legends from time to time. Now and again, someone in the burglary trade would whisper one of the old myths—that if the Candle Man crossed your path, you would soon be snuffed out."

Wind rattled the window. Chloe and Theo both jumped, then relaxed.

"We'd better go," she said.

"No, not yet!" Foley suddenly begged them. "This is my chance—to get it all out of the house!" He gave them an ingratiating grin. "I'll show you the stuff," he said. "Come down to the shop!"

CHAPTER 15

# CLOSING IN

UNKNOWN TO THE PEOPLE INSIDE THE ROOM, a gray figure was clinging to the wall outside, crouched just above the window. The thick, dirty fog concealed him from human eyes. Flin, a smoglodyte spy, had been following the events within. He scampered back up to the roof, where his leader, Skun, was awaiting his report.

"They're moving!" whispered Flin. "Reckon we should strike now!"

"Not yet," whispered Skun, the chief smoglodyte tracker. He narrowed his tiny eyes in thought, his face resembling a shrewd, shriveled turnip.

"Let's see where they go. We could learn some

secrets here." Skun wasn't like the average smoglodyte. He didn't believe in just following orders — he
wanted to know *why*. Most smogs never bothered
with that part. The tribe had been told by the illus-
trious Society of Good Works to grab Theo. Skun
had been watching this strange boy — he looked
weak, bewildered, half-asleep most of the time. Why
was he so important?

Skun crept up the rooftop and spoke to a group of
surly, wrinkled smogs huddled at the top under a
big chimney pot.

"Our target is on the move," he said. "I'll need one
of you under every ledge and above every doorway."
Skun surveyed the ragged mob. He distrusted every
one of them. He alone, the great hunter, had tracked
the boy Theo — all the way, by scent — from the
graveyard, in a slow, painstaking pursuit. He had
been forced to gather these scum along the way, as
reinforcements.

"Let's just kill him now," said Frub, a bloated old
smog. "That's what the Society really wants. It's
what it always used to want, anyway." The other
smogs leapt to their feet. They were all ready to
follow Frub. They wanted to score a quick man-kill
and then live off the reputation for years.

"They're in the downstairs shop now," reported

Flin, the spy smog, popping his head back up over the roof edge. "Make your move, Skun, or someone else will."

It was looking bad. Skun's glorious hunt for the boy—across a London that had grown to a stupendous size—should be a tale enjoyed by smoglings for years to come. *Capturing* the boy was the real task. But if this rabble didn't get to see some action soon, they would first kill Skun, then Theo—and take all the credit for the hunt.

Skun sighed. Maybe he would just let them slay the girl anyway, to keep things bright. Suddenly Frub stood in front of Skun—a clear insult—and turned to address the smog rabble.

"I say we start killing now!" he hissed. "And I'm not fussy about *who*!" Frub looked meaningfully at Skun. Then something else caught his eye, and he glanced upwards. It was the last thing he did. A dark shape dropped out of the sky and crushed him to death.

"Garghoul!" screeched Skun. The terrible creature had landed in their midst, its dark horns lowered, its eyes flashing blue fire. "Kill it!" Skun cried.

The smogs leapt on their attacker. In an old smog maneuver, they tried to wrap all their stretchy bodies around him at once, in a big ball, suffocating and crushing their foe. But this garghoul was tough. He was already breaking out of the smog-ball, ripping his foes to shreds with claw and fang. Skun backed away, down the roof.

"I am Skun, chief tracker of the Ilk tribe," he called out, trying to maintain his authority. "We are here on *human business*—which you are forbidden to interfere in!"

The garghoul ignored him. For a moment, the sheer terror of its silent presence almost overwhelmed him. There had been rumors among the smoglodytes of a shadow following them as they searched the city for Theo. Skun realized now he should have paid those rumors more attention.

A terrible battle ensued, as one by one the garghoul tore the smoglodytes apart. Soon, their shredded bodies were strewn all over the rooftop. In the thick fog, the battle went unnoticed by human eyes, and completely unsuspected by Theo below.

Skun had to forget about the mission now. He had to preserve the most valuable tribe member—himself. His smog team were managing to scratch and bruise the garghoul—even poison him with their toxic claws—but it was obvious there would be only one victor. And there was something familiar about this proud, ferocious enemy.

"It's Tristus!" Skun realized, as he began to slink away. "One of the most feared garghouls of all." There were dark legends about Tristus. Skun knew he had to take off fast.

"Help me!" squealed Flin, the little spy, crushed under one garghoul claw and about to have his throat torn out by the other. Skun didn't. With a lame smile—and a cheeky bow—he sprang off the roof and lost himself in the filthy night. Even Tristus was unable to stop him.

———•◆•———

Unaware of events on the rooftop above, Theo followed Foley into the dingy premises on the ground floor. The engraving shop had been neglected for years. Piles of yellowing prints lay discarded on tables, awaiting a restorer's hand that would now probably never come. Whole portfolios jammed with maps, diagrams, depictions of long-forgotten sea battles, and portraits of families long gone, were stacked in toppling piles. The once-prized engravings in frames on the walls were mottled with damp now, uncared for.

"Worthless rubbish," Foley muttered, gesturing at the moldy artworks. "I used to keep the old family business running, when my brother was alive,"

Foley said. "Can't ever find the time now."

Theo was almost trembling with excitement. Many of the prints were from the era when his ancestor Lord Wickland had been alive. *The lost secrets are getting nearer*, he thought, his heart racing. *The truth is getting close enough to touch.*

The old man groaned as he bent down to open a corner cupboard. It was crammed with crumpled old papers. He dragged an old biscuit tin out from under the pile and put it on a work bench.

"Grandad gave me this before he died. Wanted me to look after it, because he knew my dad had no time for the old Dodo stories." With shaking hands, the old man opened the tin. As well as a roll of paper, there were a couple of military medals, a dog collar, and a little toy soldier.

"Sentimental rubbish," Foley said quietly, tipping the keepsakes to one side. The old burglar seemed to have recovered his composure now that he was about to unburden himself. "Don't know if this is any use to you after all this time. But I want it out. Finally. All this mystery stuff has been nothing but bad luck for me ever since I first heard about it."

Foley spread out the top sheet. "Plans for a job." He grinned. "It's a bit late to stop this caper now — it happened over a hundred years ago! Grandad was asked to transport some weird animals out of a certain house and leave them in a tunnel somewhere. There was a pickup point for some pistols marked. Nothing special."

"You don't say." Chloe yawned.

"It was a crazy idea. I used to laugh about it as a kid. It was the animals—not the pistols—that was being used to kill the other gang."

"Hilarious," Chloe said.

"This first sheet is just the map Grandad was given so he wouldn't muck up the job," Foley explained. "Now here's the interesting bit!" Foley lifted up the chart and there was another, very thin sheet under it. At first glance it appeared to be a series of geometric drawings, lines, and shapes laid over each other to make a baffling pattern.

"This was found with the map. Grandad reckoned it wasn't supposed to be there. It must have been included by accident, rolled up in a careless moment by one of the bosses. Grandad said it held a great secret—never told me what."

Foley looked up, hoping for some sign of interest. He was disappointed. His mysterious visitors just stared blankly.

"Is this all you've got?" Theo asked, somewhat crestfallen. "I thought you might have pictures of the Candle Man. And I really want to read *Slaughter of the Gargoyles*!"

Chloe just sighed and carelessly stuffed all the papers back in the box.

"Might be useful to wrap our chips in," she remarked. "Come on, Theo, we've wasted enough time here. All we've got is hearsay and the plans to a hundred-year-old mugging. Might as well have spent the afternoon painting my toenails."

"Say what you like," Foley said, sulking. "Those was great secrets in their day. Meant a lot to me as a kid, being trusted with that stuff. Here, hold on!"

Foley rushed back across the room and stopped Theo in the doorway.

Theo was amazed to be loaded up with camera equipment and a laptop computer, which the burglar pulled from under a smelly blanket in a long disused dog basket.

"Here's your stuff back, Weirdy." Foley gave a cracked grin. "I passed your test, didn't I?" he said. "You was waiting to see if I'd give this lot back! No need to punish me now, is there?"

"No," said Theo simply. "You, err . . . you did the right thing."

Suddenly they were back on the streets, with Chloe hurriedly waving for a cab. Theo looked up excitedly.

"Are we really going to have chips?" he asked.

"If you like." Chloe grinned. They bundled into a taxi and sank into the deep red seats gratefully. It had been a long, tense day.

"We learned a lot," Theo remarked eagerly.

Chloe ignored him, peering at the pile of Foley's goodies balanced on her lap.

"Shame that lot turned out to be pretty useless," Theo said.

Chloe looked up, her eyes alight with excitement.

"Theo Wickland, my dear boy"—she grinned at him—"we have just hit gold dust!"

As they pulled away, neither noticed a dark, winged shape swooping away from the rooftop above.

# CHAPTER 16

# A VISITATION

THE MONSTROUS SILHOUETTE loomed in the study doorway, a hunchbacked giant of a man. A long, antiquated cape swamped his body, and a deep hood concealed his face.

"Who—who are you?" stuttered Dr. Saint, his eyes bulging behind his circular spectacles. He whirled round to call for assistance. "Mr. Nicely! Come here at once! Explain this intrusion!" he barked.

No one answered his summons. A moment before, all had seemed in order at Empire Hall. The master of the house had been sitting in his shirtsleeves, nibbling a bowl of celery, studying reams of readouts from the Mercy Tube Archive. Now suddenly he faced the unknown.

"Where is he?" the extraordinary stranger demanded in a thick, deliberate voice, as if his tongue were too big for his mouth.

Dr. Saint blinked, horrified.

"His scent is all over this place!" growled the stranger.

Dr. Saint pulled on his gray jacket and donned his bow tie smartly, pulling himself together. He would not be taken at a disadvantage, right here in Empire Hall.

"I don't believe the Society of Good Works has granted you an audience," he replied haughtily.

"I don't believe I requested one!" shouted back the intruder, stepping closer. "I want *him*!" screeched the stranger with sudden rage. "I know he has been here!"

"Who?"

"Master Luke Anderson," the figure said.

"I don't know anyone by that name," Dr. Saint said innocently, his glance flitting from the garden windows to the outside corridor, for any sign of his own staff.

The stranger drew closer. Dr. Saint was starting to get a glimpse of the face concealed in the hood, and it was not a welcome sight.

"Let's try another name," said the visitor quietly. "Wickland!" he suddenly roared, making Dr. Saint jump, despite his best efforts to remain composed. "Now you know what I mean, don't you, you craven, two-faced hypocrite! I'm looking for Wickland, son of Wickland, son of Wickland, *son of Wickland*!" he bellowed. "I think I've got that right," he added, finally calm again.

"Who—who are you?" Dr. Saint asked. The stranger threw back his hood. Dr. Saint struggled to regain his composure as he saw the hideously deformed head, the immense, crooked nose, the dark, sunken eyes.

"I am known to you people as the Dodo," he breathed. Dr. Saint stepped back. The dreadful face combined with an unearthly body odor almost caused him to faint.

"You—you can't be him!" Dr. Saint said finally.

The intruder's face was disfigured by a bitter smile. "Unfortunately for me, the Dodo is the only person I *can* be," he said darkly.

"This is impossible!" blurted out Dr. Saint, dashing behind his desk in a sudden panic. "Mr. Nicely! Foundlings! In here at once!" He began to scrabble in a drawer for a revolver he kept hidden there, but he was knocked down by a vicious claw.

Dr. Saint tried to rise, but he was trodden to the ground by an enormous boot. A gnarled, twisted hand appeared from the folds of the Dodo's great cloak, snatched Dr. Saint's gun from the drawer, and clung on to it with talonlike fingers.

"Your associates will not be coming to help you," the Dodo said. Then he barked out a single, guttural command and looked towards the door. From his position, still lying on the floor, Dr. Saint followed the gaze and saw a human skull come rolling through the study door, bright white bone glistening.

It was being rolled along playfully by an outlandish beast the size of a rottweiller, yet more like a beaver in appearance. The skull still had patches of flesh and hair on it here and there. The beaver looked up quizzically at Dr. Saint, grooming its bloodied fur contentedly.

"M-Mr. Nicely?" stammered Dr. Saint, staring in horror at the skull which seemed to grin back up at him.

"Sorry, sir," said Mr. Nicely, walking into the room with his hands on his head. He was followed by Lord Dove, Lady Blessing, the skinny new maid Veracity, and two huge—but scared-looking—men in blue overalls. They were being shepherded by two more antediluvian beavers and a pair of big black rats.

"That—that should have been me," Mr. Nicely said, nodding towards the skull on the floor, which was being given a fresh lick by a beaver. "It was Masters—Lord Dove's man. I'm afraid he got to the front door first. The . . . err, rest of him's still in the hall."

"Perhaps the next time I come to call, I will receive a kinder welcome," growled the Dodo. He motioned for Dr. Saint to get up and peered closely at his face.

"You're obviously not the *real* Philanthropist," he remarked, as if disappointed. "He had a much more cultured air." Dr. Saint said nothing. "You're just the current incumbent of the position, I expect," the Dodo mused.

"I am Doctor Emmanuel Saint, head of the Society of Good Works," the Master of Empire Hall said. "But *you* can't be the Dodo!"

"He does have all the, err . . . animals," said Lady Blessing, white as a sheet.

"Animals!" snorted the Dodo. "A word invented by humans to make themselves feel superior to their fellow . . . beings. Well, you vile specimens of homo sapiens are certainly no better than my charming trogontheriums." He bent to pat one of the beaver-like creatures.

"But you—I mean he—must have been dead for years!" protested Dr. Saint. "The Dodo was last seen in nineteen oh-one!"

"Would that I *had* died in nineteen oh-one, as the world believed. But it was not . . . allowed."

"Not *allowed*?" echoed Dr. Saint, with a sudden eager interest. "Not allowed by whom?"

"By someone you know, and I know," replied the Dodo. "Oh yes, he shut down my operations—most of them—and allowed me to hide in shameful obscurity. There, away from the eyes of the world—and the underworld—I even managed to cure myself of my grotesque affliction for a while."

There was a sudden crunch as one of the trogontheriums began to chew some of the gristle around the skull's jaw.

"But then yesterday afternoon, he returned—or at least his latest descendant did. He walked into my home and he did *this* to me!" The Dodo gestured at his extraordinary face with his talonlike hand.

"Speak!" roared the Dodo suddenly, spinning round to face the assembled representatives of the Society of Good Works. "My servants know he has been here. Where is he?"

"He's escaped!" blurted out Lady Blessing. "We had him here—for a while," she said evasively. "But he was taken. By the Society of Unrelenting Vigilance!"

The Dodo looked thoughtful. He sat in Dr. Saint's best leather chair and surveyed the room. A dark cloud seemed to settle on his brow.

"The Candle Man was destroyed," the Dodo said. "But his archenemies took his bloodline. The Society of Good Works took steps to provide for Wickland's only heir. Oh yes, I've kept my eye on you, in my own way, for years. Years in which I had no power to confront you. For decades, for three generations, you manipulated events, watched over the Wickland descendants, waiting to see if the genetic line would produce another Candle Man. You finally, and very *charitably*, became the guardians of the house of Wickland. But why?"

"We simply don't want him to use his powers against us," said Dr. Saint smoothly. The Dodo scowled. The giant rats squealed and started to circle Dr. Saint slowly.

"You don't like this one, do you?" said the Dodo to his creatures.

Dr. Saint blanched.

"No," sighed the Dodo, turning away from his

145

captives. "There's more to it than that." He strode towards the door, and his creatures fell in line behind him. He stopped in the doorway, crushed the barrel of Dr. Saint's gun with his claw, and let it fall to the ground.

"The Dodo is the greatest enemy of the Candle Man," he said. "Wickland is mine. If you recapture him, hand him over to me — alive. Or you will all be thrown into my pits to die screaming!"

"Yes, sir!" squeaked Lord Dove.

But the Dodo was already disappearing down the bloody hallway.

The dead servant, Masters, had been put — bit by bit — into a body bag.

"Now get those idiots out of here," snapped Dr. Saint to Mr. Nicely, nodding towards Lord Dove and Lady Blessing. "And get this place cleaned up!"

"I'll call those Good-As-New Carpets people again," offered Mr. Nicely.

"No, you won't, you moron, this is human blood!" screamed Dr. Saint. Mr. Nicely stepped back. He noticed that his employer's hands were trembling slightly.

"I'll do it," piped up Veracity, the new maid. She smiled, revealing braces on her teeth. "I'm good with blood." She darted off towards the kitchens.

"And fumigate my study!" Dr. Saint yelled after her.

Still shaking with emotion, he strode straight into Theo's old room, which was now covered with wires and machinery everywhere. The bottom section of the Mercy Tube had been opened right up, revealing all its innards—a tangle of leads, sockets, and circuits.

"Nice cup of chamomile, sir?" suggested the butler.

Dr. Saint smiled a ghostly smile.

"I'm afraid we've reached a point in our affairs when a cup of chamomile tea can no longer solve our problems," he said. He sat on a swivel chair in front of the Mercy Tube and buried his face in his hands. Then he looked up, and there was a wild look in his eyes.

"It is not appropriate," Dr. Saint said quietly, through gritted teeth, "for the Master of Empire Hall to be hurled around like a rag doll!" Mr. Nicely had never seen his employer so consumed with rage.

"And it is not appropriate for a man who holds so much power, to be so . . . utterly powerless!" he shouted. Mr. Nicely couldn't help glancing at the cupboard where the special medicines were.

"The Liberation is nearly upon us!" Dr. Saint raved, now striding back and forth. "The Candle Man is out there eluding every attempt to catch him! Now the Dodo, the most terrible fiend of the Victorian age, has been reborn! And guess what? He doesn't like us!"

Dr. Saint stood still, gave Mr. Nicely a strange, sad look, and pointed at the door. "Get out, please!" he said. "Get out and don't let anyone in!"

Mr. Nicely fled.

Dr. Saint read and reread the years of data from the archive. By the time he was finished, the floor was a sea of paper and wires. He reversed connections, unplugged and plugged leads, reset dials, and activated the second generator.

When at last he was ready, he programmed the controls and pressed the switch to full power with a five-second delay.

Then he stepped into the Mercy Tube.

CHAPTER 17

# THE BIG PICTURE

"DON'T!" CHLOE SCREAMED, as Theo appeared to be stepping off the pavement into the path of a truck.

"I wasn't going to," Theo protested.

"With *you*, Theo, it's quite hard to tell *what* you're going to do!" Chloe remarked. "Or what you *have been doing* . . . ," she added darkly.

They watched the traffic rush by in the evening drizzle. It was nearly six o'clock. They were south of the River Thames, by Southwark Bridge, and almost at their destination.

"You're still cross I didn't tell you I'd used my powers." Theo sighed.

"Yes. Not bothering to mention that you can melt people was a pretty big omission."

"Well, I only melted Brady by accident. I don't know if I'll ever be able to do it again," Theo said. "I didn't want you and Sam thinking of me as some kind of hero. Or even worse—as some kind of horrible killer."

Chloe suddenly grinned. "If you really are going to be a great hero," she said, "I'm going to have to teach you how to cross the road—otherwise your career probably won't last very long."

"I've never really had to do it before," apologized Theo, as Chloe accompanied him to the other pavement.

Southwark Cathedral lay before them, almost lost among the more modern buildings that had sprung up around it across the centuries.

"Why do we have to come here?" Theo asked.

Chloe smiled and held up Foley's secret map.

"I really shouldn't let you in so close to closing time," a flustered lady church warden said as they stepped into the arched doorway.

"So kind of you!" gushed Chloe with a great big smile, dragging Theo behind her. She dropped some coins loudly in the donation box.

"Now let's get lost!" Chloe hissed. She hurried

Theo down the far aisle, out of sight of the main entrance. After a moment's thought, she pushed open a wooden door that led into a secluded den usually reserved for the cathedral organist. She indicated to Theo to sit down—and not to touch the keyboard. They sat in the gloom, not stirring, as gradually the footsteps and muted conversations of other visitors faded away. Not long afterwards the lights began to go off, one by one.

"We're closing!" called a distant voice, but half-heartedly, as if not really expecting any response. A door was bolted. A lock clicked, echoing throughout the vaulted chamber.

"She's shutting us in!" Theo whispered.

"That's the idea," Chloe replied. "She probably thinks we went out through the gift shop. Now come on."

Theo crept out of hiding and surveyed the enormous shadowy cathedral. Wooden cherubs peered at him from carved stalls. Effigies of dead knights slumbered on great slabs of stone.

"Spoo-oo-ky!" said Chloe in a deep voice.

Theo looked around sharply. "Why are you saying that?" he asked. "And why are you doing that silly voice?"

"I'm trying to scare you, you big twit," Chloe said. "It's what friends do."

151

Theo felt a secret glow at being considered a friend by this remarkable and dangerous person.

"Well, I'm sufficiently scared about things already, if you hadn't noticed," he replied. "I saw three smoglodytes and two giant rats on the way here. Lucky we were in a bus."

"Those were Yorkshire terriers. You're just imagining things."

Chloe opened her backpack. The cameras and laptop from Empire Hall were still inside. So was a giant salami roll they had picked up on the journey over. Chloe tore it in two and gave Theo the bigger bit. Then she took a silver candlestick from a nearby lectern and lit it. She and Theo sat in the deserted choir stalls. With great care, she unrolled the hundred-year-old chart Foley had given them.

"This is the good bit," said Chloe. "Now pay attention." She held the bright flame up close to the paper. Theo saw the colored jumble of lines.

"What do you think it is?" Chloe asked.

Theo frowned. "Some sort of machine," he ventured.

Chloe laughed. "Look again," she said. "See these blue lines here—do they remind you of anything?"

"Pipes. Plumbing. I don't know. There's a big space in the middle. And something like an island.

It's a treasure map!" He beamed, remembering one of his favorite stories.

Chloe laughed again. "You're just guessing wildly, but you're getting warmer. Now look here—" She stopped talking, and Theo was amazed to see she was almost overcome with excitement. She gulped and carried on. "This is Clapham Junction."

"A London train station." Theo smiled.

"Yes, except this isn't the real Clapham Junction. It's just a name we give to a busy part of the network. I took you through here when we were escaping from the Dodo. And here's the gulag—the prison bit. We call it that because that's the scary bit where the Eighty-eight are locked up. Or not—depending on what you believe."

It was a slight drawback in the outside world, Theo reflected, that the more excited people got, the harder they were to understand. But he had learned to be patient.

"Err—wow!" he said, politely showing an interest in other people's enthusiasms. "A map of the network! Didn't you have one already?"

"Of course we did—the *known* network. But look at these lines in red and purple and green. . . ."

"What are they?"

Chloe looked up, her face glowing. "They clearly

show *other* tunnels—lower down! A sort of under-network, if you like. Whole hidden pathways that we had no idea existed." She held the bright flame closer to the chart.

"It's kind of hard to make out," she admitted, "because of all the different colors. But what it reveals is that the network has a weird—well, a symmetry!"

"Which means . . . ?"

"That our history is wrong! The network isn't just a few drainage schemes from the Victorian times cobbled together to make secret passages. This map proves that the whole system was *planned*. It's older than we ever guessed. And it probably has a purpose we've never guessed either."

"And we're here," said Theo, pointing at a stenciled cathedral shape on the blue part of the map. "But how do we find the secret entrance?"

"We bring someone clever along—me!" said Chloe. And she led him into the crypt.

———— ◆ ————

A faint halo of light dispelled decades of darkness as the circular hatchway appeared in the crypt wall.

"How did you know where it was?" asked Theo as they stepped inside.

"There are formulas, protocols. In the old times

buildings were constructed to contain messages. I can *read* this crypt the same way you can read a book," Chloe said with a hint of pride.

"And why are we going in here?" Theo asked. "I'm not completely clear on that."

"Because of this map," Chloe replied. "Fate has put it in our hands. Now we know how the Society of Good Works always got away from us in the past—they had extra secret tunnels. Well, now we can turn the tables. We can use this map to spy on them. You heard what Sergeant Crane said: if I don't find evidence of what the enemy are up to soon, the police are going to drop the whole case."

A narrow, arched tunnel delved deep under the cathedral. Theo noticed that the fungus globes here seemed almost dead, giving only a spark of organic light. Maybe this route had lain unused for decades.

"Suppose they aren't up to anything?" Theo asked.

"Don't be dense!" Chloe exploded. "They sent those smogs out to snatch you! They smashed up the cottage. They're on the war path!" She gave Theo a withering look.

"Norrowmore knew they were up to something big," she continued. "He wanted you rescued before it all kicked off! I was never told the big picture—I was too low down in our Society to be trusted with all the Mysteries. But now we're the only ones left, and we have to find out what's going on!"

Theo fell silent. He desperately hoped they weren't the only ones left and clung to the belief that Sam and Magnus had escaped somehow. Chloe led the way, striding through the near-darkness with confidence. Theo kept up with her as best he could. After about an hour, she halted in an archway up ahead.

"Are we stopping for a rest?" asked Theo hopefully.

"We can have a nice long rest when we're dead," said Chloe. "Take a look at this!"

"What is it?"

*What is it, what is it . . . ?* Theo's voice echoed through the gloom.

"It's the Holy Grail!" Chloe whispered. "Well, better than that—it's our own private route into the heart of enemy territory!"

They had emerged into a vast spherical stone chamber as wide as the cathedral they had left behind. They were standing on an iron platform that connected with a central spiral stairway that seemed to go down forever.

"Take a deep breath, Theo—this is where the real adventure starts," Chloe said. "We're stepping into the unknown."

Theo gazed into the blackness below. Who knew

what terrors lay down there? *This is it,* he thought. *If ever I'm going to back out, it has to be now.*

Chloe grinned up at him.

"Come on, Weirdy!" she teased. "You'll be right at home!"

"Aren't you scared?" asked Theo.

"Not really," said Chloe. "I've got the Candle Man with me. Now follow me — we're going all the way to the bottom."

Theo's heart was in his mouth. Did Chloe *really* expect him to be some kind of hero now, just because he was the great-great-great-grandson of Lord Wickland? Just because he had melted somebody once — by accident? Theo had believed he was a feeble invalid from Day One of his life. He wasn't used to people having expectations of him — especially heroic ones. It was extremely unsettling.

Down they went, their feet echoing on the ancient stairway. Icy drips fell on them from above as they trod the iron steps, round and round, ever downward in the darkness. It was like moving in a dream, beyond your own control. Theo felt he had left his younger, more cautious self forever waiting and wondering at the top of the stairs — while a mad new Theo was plunging ahead, running on pure hope.

Mr. Nicely had told Theo a childish riddle once.

*How far can a dog run into a wood?* The silly answer had been: *Halfway. Because after that he's running out.* Theo felt like he was running into a dark wood now. The wood was getting darker and more frightening all the time. But if he continued to run, there might be a point—there had to be a point—when he was running out, back into the light. That was the hope he clung to, as he kept moving onward.

Finally there were no more stairs. The exhausted pair found themselves in a cavern that stretched before them for miles. Mist lay as thick as cobwebs over the stinking mire that filled the underground chamber.

As far as the eye could see the dreary wreck of some ancient cataclysm met the eye. Whole tree trunks lay moldering in black heaps; there were piles of unnameable debris, drowned machinery, the skeleton of a horse. An enormous, shattered fungus globe lay like a broken water lily in the center of the floods, its glowing contents creeping out across the swamp, shedding a livid glow.

The two figures straggled across the mire, wallowing through the waters with grim determination.

"Where are we?" wondered Theo.

"The bottom," said Chloe simply. "Something terrible must have happened down here—long ago."

"It looks like the end of the world," said Theo.

They sloshed forward through the reeking slime, casting bright ripples of bioluminesence.

"My feet hurt," complained Theo. The water was loosening his half-healed blisters, making them rub all over again.

"Well? My whole *me* hurts," retorted Chloe. "I've been fighting the so-called Society of Good Works ever since I was six. Always on the losing side, always buying flowers for more graves. An endless slog against an enemy who always knows more than you do."

Theo decided not to mention his feet again for a bit. But Chloe's frown changed into a smile.

"It's different now, though," she said. "We've got you. For the first time ever, the tide is turning."

The mire was getting shallower now, as they reached the center of the chamber.

"But—" Theo began, then stopped and stared glumly ahead.

"But what?"

"Well, it's just you and me, isn't it?" he said slowly. "The big things in this world—like, I don't know, wars or . . . or the Ascendancy—those big things just happen, don't they? People like us can't do anything about it."

Chloe plodded grimly onwards, her cap concealing her gaze, her black dress growing sodden.

"Do you really believe," Theo pressed, "that just one or two people—like you and me—can actually change things? Make something . . . good happen?"

"Unluckily for me, Theo," Chloe said, "that's exactly what I *do* believe. Wait—take a look at this!"

The mists thinned out as they stepped onto dry land. They had reached an island in the mire, from which dark stone slabs arose, each marking a sinister mound. There were hundreds of these, in straight rows, vanishing off into the distance.

Almost against their will, Theo and Chloe were drawn to a large monument in the center. A familiar figure was carved into it, like a winged demon with curled horns, hooked nose, staring human eyes, and a grim mouth.

Chloe started trying to count the mysterious gravestones. She soon gave up.

"All the horrible stories turned out to be true," Chloe muttered, half recalling the words of the robber, Foley. "Something bad happened here. And I feel like it's not yet over," she added in a whisper.

Theo climbed up and peered into the dead eyes of the carved figure on the monument. Now he knew what this place reminded him of—one of Foley's grandad's long-lost storybooks.

*"Slaughter of the Gargoyles,"* Theo said.

160

# CHAPTER 18

# FLIGHTS

RISTUS THE GARGHOUL AWOKE to find tiny silver mice creeping around at his feet. This was a peculiar — and worrying — development. Usually the other creatures in his lair ignored him, as if he were just a piece of stone. Now he had attracted a most unwelcome thing: curiosity.

He was hurt, tired, barely able to think. He groaned inwardly as it all came back to him — the fight with the smoglodytes on the roof. He had protected the boy but been badly clawed and poisoned. He had made it back to his refuge in the Dodo's cavern and entered his stone dream to give his body time to heal.

The little mice beneath him became excited and started to dart around, squeaking. Moments later, a pair of big black rats loped into view, brushing the mice aside and sniffing suspiciously along the rock ledge the garghoul had called home for almost a century.

The rats lifted their snouts, sat back on their haunches, and let out a high-pitched whine, horrible to hear but mercifully brief. Soon after, heavy keys clattered and snapped at locks, and the metal doors crashed open. A crooked human shape loomed over the garghoul. A bony Caspian tiger lurked behind him.

"Something has changed," growled the Dodo, inspecting Tristus closely. "This is not the dull, dead creature I recall!"

Tristus kept his eyes closed and remained as still as only a garghoul can. The Dodo crouched down and faced Tristus with a deep sigh.

"You were supposed to be the pride of my collection," the Dodo said at length. "When I rescued you from the ruins of the network a hundred years ago, I considered you my greatest discovery. But you became my biggest disappointment. Never waking, never speaking! Never opening those fabled eyes."

Tristus could hear the bitterness—loneliness, even—in the Dodo's voice. But garghouls do not choose to communicate with many mortals, and he remained silent.

"You're not a statue, sir!" the Dodo said. "Living creatures have been my lifelong study, and a living thing is undoubtedly what you are. Your demeanor has changed—you are somehow . . . alert."

The tiger licked at the black, damp drizzle of guts on the rock ledge, which had caused such interest amongst the rodents. The Dodo bent down with an awkward lurch to sniff the spot.

"You've been eating too!" he said, his eyes aglow with intrigue. He slapped the tiger on the haunch, and it slunk away obediently. He ran his fingers through the curious straggle of wet innards and lifted them up to his nostrils.

"Smoglodytes," he murmured, rising slowly. "This paints a more dangerous picture." The rodents, sensing their master's excitement, scurried to his side. The tiger rumbled a deep-throated growl.

Tristus tried to pull his muddled wits together. His human visitor was not the sleepy, bored old man who had been shambling through these caverns for decades. Sir Peregrine had become charged with a new intensity—a new power. The garghoul knew he had now lost his safe, quiet lair.

"Dr. Saint must have struck a deal with the smoglodytes!" the Dodo muttered. "No wonder the Society of Good Works struts about this city with such confounded arrogance!"

The Dodo suddenly grabbed Tristus and stretched out one of his batlike wings. The leathery skin was freshly scarred, partially torn.

"You've been out there—I knew I could smell it on you. I expect the smoglodytes gave you these souvenirs," the Dodo added. A mixture of anger and dismay contorted his features. "You're awake! Confound you, sir—I *know* you're awake!"

*Time to go*, Tristus said to himself.

"Why?" the Dodo roared. "Why won't you speak?"

The garghoul rose. The Dodo staggered back.

"A—a hundred years without motion, and now you stand before me!" the astonished man exclaimed. A tiny glitter of light, like stardust, appeared in the garghoul's narrowed eyes.

"You're involved in all these events, aren't you?" the Dodo whispered in awe. "I know you can speak—tell me what's going on!"

The garghoul sprang into the air, beat its powerful wings, and disappeared into the shadows of the ceiling.

———————

"It's dead down here," Chloe said. "There's nothing more we can learn. Come on, let's try another level." She pointed upwards.

They retraced their steps, glad to get away from the eerie graveyard. Halfway back across the mire, Theo stopped next to a colossal upturned tree root and glanced back. He clutched at Chloe and pointed over the mists. There, on the memorial where they had so recently stood, was the impish silhouette of a smoglodyte.

"That was close!" Chloe hissed. They backpedaled behind the tree root and stared. The single figure sprang up, waving its arms wildly. In moments the memorial stone was swarming with smoglodytes.

"What are they doing?" Theo wondered nervously.

"It's sweet the way you think I know everything," snapped Chloe. "How the heck do I know? They aren't there to lay flowers, that's for sure!"

For a horrible moment Theo had the impression the swarm of smoglodytes was heading their way. Then he was certain of it — they were.

"Come on!" he said, wading away as fast as he could. Chloe didn't need any persuading. The mist over the mire hid them pretty well, but there was no point in taking chances. They struggled back to the foot of the great stairway.

"Straight up," Chloe ordered. They ascended, their wet clothes weighing them down. After a few minutes, Theo peered out across the vapors and was sure he could see tiny heads, bobbing up and down, a whole troop of smoglodytes heading towards the staircase.

"They're on to us!" he called up to Chloe. "What now?"

"We keep climbing!" she said.

Theo felt sick. He had collapsed onto his knees on the second landing. This was the level he and Chloe had used before, to escape from the Dodo. Chloe listened at the circular hatchway.

"Let's get in here. I know it like the back of my hand. I'll find a place to rest up before we do any more spying! The Society of Good Works might even have a cafeteria down here. We can disguise ourselves and get a bacon sandwich."

Theo knew she was joking, trying to make him forget his exhaustion. She made a last, vain attempt to listen through the hatchway, then opened a glass pane over the central plaque that activated the door.

For a moment Theo thought his eyes were playing tricks on him, but a steady gaze removed all doubt. Even through his thick gloves, Theo's hands had started to glow faintly.

"Don't open it!" he hissed. "There must be somebody on the other side!"

It was too late. Chloe had already activated the hatch.

The shaven-headed brute of a guard looked shocked as the doorway sprang open, revealing two bedraggled intruders. He pulled a gun from a shoulder holster, but Chloe leapt through the hatch, grabbed his wrist, and smashed his hand against the wall. The guard cried out but did not drop his gun. He grabbed Chloe with his free hand and hurled her to the floor.

Theo threw himself through the hatchway. The guard swung a fist and smashed Theo back through the hatch without taking his eyes off Chloe, whom he had identified as the dangerous one of the two. Theo stumbled to his feet and tore off his gauntlets. A flicker of pale fire played around his fingers. Theo gulped. Was he really going to use his terrible power again? Would it even work for him this time?

Chloe was trying to struggle to her feet, but a

ruthless boot sent her sprawling back across the ground. Theo, climbing back through the hatch, saw a trickle of blood on her cheek.

Theo stared with horror at the brutality of the guard as he fought Chloe. It was now or never. Concentrating on his hands, he tried to summon the power. He dug deep into his heart and mind, like a runner asking his body for a final effort in a desperate race. Suddenly his fingers began to burn brightly with a ghostly flame.

"Bad luck, lady," the guard growled. "Orders from the top say don't bother taking any prisoners!"

He raised his gun. But he never pulled the trigger. Theo had dived forward and touched the guard's trailing fingers. The Foundling froze like a statue. His body became engulfed in a green glow. Two bulging eyes stared in terror before they melted and flowed down the man's cheeks. The heavy blue overalls bubbled, shredded, and streamed away. The gun clattered to the ground. The Foundling was soon a pool of warm pink slime on the tunnel floor.

"Oh, wow," Chloe gasped, staring at the smoking remains. She then swore, using several words that Theo had never heard before.

"Nice one, Theo. Now I can see why Foley was so scared of you," she whispered. She wiped blood away from her lip, tossed her hair out of her face.

"I mean, hearing about it is one thing—actually seeing it is another. . . ."

Theo looked away from the guard's smoking remains. Grim-faced, he pulled his gloves back on.

"Perhaps you can see now why I wanted to keep it secret for as long as possible," Theo said anxiously. "I mean, even someone as brave and crazy as you isn't going to want to hang out with a freak who can melt people to death!" Instead of feeling triumphant after the fight, he just felt miserable.

"Nonsense, Theo," Chloe said, pulling herself together. "In fact, you're just the kind of friend a brave and crazy person like me needs." She smiled, and for the first time in a very long time, Theo felt as if everything was going to be all right.

"And don't worry," Chloe added. "What else could you do? Would you rather *we* were both lying here dead?" She closed the hatch and looked around with her habitual caution.

"No wonder you're such big news." Chloe's mind was racing. "A boy born with a real-life death touch. If the Society of Good Works could study—maybe replicate—your power, the world would be in serious trouble."

"Well, don't forget they put me in that Mercy

Tube every day. You must have seen that on your spying missions at Empire Hall."

"Of course!" Chloe gasped. "I guess the world must already be in serious trouble." She started to pace ahead into the darkness. "Thanks for saving my life, by the way." She grinned, glancing back over her shoulder.

***

They were unlucky. The network was no longer the quiet catacomb Chloe had so often slipped through before. Now it was a hive of activity. Chloe knew how to keep to the shadows, but there were precious few shadows left. Arc lights, rigged to mobile generators, shone brightly on scenes of great industry. Chemicals were being unpacked by Foundling slaves, measured by Society scientists, supervised by members of the Board.

One of the underground canals that had been disused for decades was now busy with small boats laden with drums of chemicals. Chloe noted that a team of Foundlings was pouring sacks of a pale gray powder straight into the water.

"What are they up to?" she wondered. Drawn by all this enemy activity like a moth to a flame, Chloe sneaked in too close to discover what the chemicals were. She was spotted, her shadow thrown against a cavern wall by one of the electric lamps.

"Intruders!" squawked the hysterical voice of Lord Dove. "Get them!"

Chloe cursed. "Retreat!" She tried to lead Theo back the way they had come, but a group of armed guards was marching down from that direction.

Theo's hands flickered with light. Chloe grabbed him by the coat and dragged him down a side passage.

"We'll be okay," she panted. "There's always a secondary hatch close to a major doorway." She soon spotted what she was looking for up ahead.

"Open it!" shouted Theo, hearing echoing footsteps getting nearer. But the hatch was welded shut, sprayed with a red *L*, and adorned with a bar-code sticker.

"What are they doing?" she cried out. Now there was only one other way to go. "Follow me and don't look back," Chloe said. She sprinted down the passage to their left. It opened out into a long brick tunnel, with a culvert of black water trickling down the middle. "Faster!" she shrieked, as an earsplitting crack reverberated around them and a bullet whined off the brickwork nearby. They rounded a corner, momentarily safe from attack.

"Oh, no!" Chloe gasped. She was staring at the tunnel ahead. It was bricked up, with fresh mortar dribbling from the cracks, and was also sprayed with an *L*.

"What *is* that?" Chloe gasped. "What does *L* stand for?" Now she led Theo down the only remaining tunnel, running along a narrow ledge above the increasingly wide black stream.

"We're heading towards the main canal," she shouted. "On the borders of the gulag!" Theo recalled she had mentioned the gulag before, but its significance escaped him. Another bullet ricocheted through the tunnel, burying itself in a wall not far behind them.

"This is it!" said Chloe as they reached a pair of archways. "All we have to do is —" She stopped dead. Marching footsteps were echoing down one of the two ways ahead. Coming towards them.

"That sounds like a lot of people!" Theo said, dismayed. His hands were luminous with pale green flame, but he knew in his heart that he could never take on such a large enemy force.

"Faster!" shrieked a familiar voice from down the tunnel. "We can cut them off if we're quick!"

Theo felt his stomach churn. That voice belonged to Dr. Saint.

"Okay, so we go this way," Chloe said, a strange look of resignation on her face. She pointed Theo to the black mouth of the only tunnel left available to them. Theo was surprised when Chloe reached out and held him by his gloved left hand.

"Don't be afraid," she said.

"Why should I—or shouldn't I—be afraid?" Theo asked in his smallest voice.

Chloe spoke in a reverent hush. "This is the way into the gulag. Home of the Eighty-eight. Nobody sane goes down here. Ever. But look on the bright side," she added as they plunged into the darkness. "Our enemies *won't* be following us."

# CHAPTER 19

# THE EIGHTY-EIGHT

HEY'RE DEAD, sir."

The party of Foundling guards stood grimly before the tunnel entrance. Dr. Saint received the news calmly, a cold glint in his eye.

"Who is responsible for this act of ultimate kindness?" he asked.

"*They* are," replied Captain Hope, the leader of the guards. He was an ex-soldier, tall, red-faced, with narrow gray eyes. He saluted Dr. Saint, army style. "The intruders have doomed themselves. They were caught between my group and yours. It was certain death or capture—so they chose that tunnel, sir. Went into the gulag."

"Was there a definite identification?" asked Mr. Nicely, cutting a slightly quaint figure in his Wellington boots. "No chance of a mistake?"

"No—it was the Vessel. I can confirm it myself," Lord Dove said.

"I tried to wound the other one," Captain Hope added, "the female agent who was with him—but she knows the network too well. They escaped and fled down there."

Everyone's eyes turned to the forbidden tunnel. Dr. Saint drew Lord Dove to one side.

"Theo wouldn't know about this death trap!" observed Dr. Saint. "But she . . . ?"

"Hard to say," commented Lord Dove. "We know little about her. So far, most of our agents sent to intercept the pair have been killed or hospitalized. We think she's part of Norrowmore's 'Modern Vigilance.' He may not have told her anything about the old days, the wars, the Eighty-eight . . . You know how secretive he always was."

"So they came down here to spy on us and accidentally ran into the one place they couldn't possibly survive." Dr. Saint reflected, with a hint of satisfaction. This tragic event was not without its convenient side. In the last ten years he had ordered several expeditions into the gulag in an attempt to clear the

175

Eighty-eight out. Not a single one of his men had ever returned alive.

"She was a very smart agent," Lord Dove said. "Knew our tunnels pretty well. But the preparations for the Liberation caught her completely off guard. Remember—we've sealed nearly all the hatches, as you directed."

Lord Dove's face was drained, full of anxiety, even though he was reporting excellent news. A little nerve was pulsing under his left eye. His violet bow tie was slightly askew after the unaccustomed chase through the tunnels, and his white suit was splashed with filthy water from the culvert.

"What's the matter, Dove?" Dr. Saint asked sharply. "You seem distressed by this turn of events."

"Well, if the Vessel has passed beyond us," Lord Dove began, eyeing the black mouth of the tunnel, "then isn't the Liberation rather, err . . . off?"

"Poppycock," said Dr. Saint. "The power of the Vessel has been sampled, analyzed, and re-created by science." He loomed over his colleague. "I performed the transfer myself, in the Mercy Tube," he revealed. "The power is now contained in *me*!"

Lord Dove looked pale. "Do you—do you realize what this means?" he stammered.

"What's the matter, Dove?" Dr. Saint asked. "Shocked at my initiative? In awe at my boldness? Of course I know what it means! After all these years of awaiting the return of the Candle Man, I have handed him his ultimate defeat—I have *become* him!"

Lord Dove went white and staggered backwards, away from the triumphant figure of his leader.

"Dr. Saint?" said Mr. Nicely, stepping smartly between his employer and the cowering Lord Dove.

"What is it, Mr. Nicely? Why must I be interrupted? Confound you, man!"

Mr. Nicely made an apologetic bow. "Sorry, sir, but I thought you might like to know. Your face is melting."

———◆———

"Okay, now I can't see *anything*," Theo whispered. Not a glimmer of light penetrated from the corridor they had left. The pair were in pitch-blackness; only the echoes of their footsteps told them they were surrounded by the usual stone walls.

"Don't whisper," said Chloe loudly, still holding Theo's hand. "Ghosts *like* that. It gives them more power. We have to act as if we're in broad daylight.

I think we can get through here alive if we don't let this place mess with our minds!"

"So are the Eighty-eight *ghosts*?" Theo asked, feeling his way by running his free hand along the rough stone wall. He had never been in total blackness before, and it was not a welcome experience.

"I don't know for sure," Chloe said. "As usual, old Norrowmore kept me in the dark."

"Good one," interrupted Theo.

"That's the spirit," Chloe said. "Keep your morale up. I have managed to glean a few clues. There were terrible events down in these tunnels once. The Eighty-eight were victims, I think—left down here to die. They died all right, but they didn't exactly . . . go away."

Theo felt a sense of dread creeping over him.

*Crunch*. Theo stepped on something brittle. Chloe struck a flame from a cheap lighter in her pocket. It was very low on fuel.

"Human bone," she said, studying the remains. "Shin, I think." They crept forwards. Theo's feet clattered against something metallic. Chloe struck another light, saw a gun, and picked it up.

"Police specialist firearm: Heckler and Koch semi-automatic. About five years old. That's interesting." She sounded flat. "Norrowmore warned me the

Society of Good Works might also have connections in the police."

Theo's toes kicked another collection of bones.

"Okay," Chloe said, with forced casualness. "This is a crushed human skull. Compacted from all sides at once. Hard to do, but effective. Nice."

"Ghosts don't crush skulls," Theo said. "From what I've read in my storybooks, spooks scare, they don't kill."

"The Eighty-eight might," Chloe said quietly, laying the gun back by its owner's side.

"Shouldn't we keep that?"

"Well, it didn't do these guys any good, did it?" Chloe replied. "Anyway, it's out of ammo. Whoever these people were, they died in here firing off all the shots they had left. It didn't help."

Chloe's lighter suddenly sputtered and ran out of fuel. Theo quickly grabbed her hand, not wanting to be alone in the dark. They crept slowly along, Chloe feeling the wall to her left.

"We'll come to something soon," she reassured Theo. "An old fungus globe, or a shaft letting in light from above. Just you wait. Trust me—I'm good with tunnels, I—"

Chloe suddenly screamed. She plunged downwards, letting go of Theo's hand.

"Chloe!" Theo cried. There was no reply. She had been swallowed up by the dark. He cried her name out once more. Again there was no reply. Fear clutched at his heart. He was left standing alone in utter blackness. He stood still, afraid to move. He had to remain safe — he mustn't disappear like she had.

He took a deep breath and called her name over and over again. The echoes resounded mockingly. It seemed to take forever for the last whispers to fade away. Even then, Theo seemed to hear her name replaying itself over and over in his tired brain. *Chloeee.*

Finally he gave up. Shouting and screaming wouldn't do any good. He had to keep his head or all was lost. He needed information — he needed to know where she had disappeared to. Slowly he sank down onto his knees. He felt along the ground in the darkness and his fingers came to a ledge — a hole or shaft in the floor. Chloe had stepped right into it, that much was clear. But where was she now, and what on earth was Theo going to do?

For a moment he gave in to despair and buried his face in his hands. Desperately, he fought back panic. *It's happened*, Theo thought. *I'm alone.*

*Alone*, he reflected. How often, during his incarceration at Empire Hall had he craved to be out here, in the real world, on his own, making his own decisions—free. Now his wish had been granted in the most terrible circumstances imaginable.

For a moment he let the dread overcome him. He knelt, waiting for something awful to happen to him, but it didn't. He expected the Eighty-eight to come and rip the flesh from his bones. That didn't happen either. His thoughts began to clear. *At least I'm still alive. It's not over yet.*

He didn't want to let Chloe down; he didn't want to let the Society of Unrelenting Vigilance down. He thought of Sam and Magnus—how much they had risked to help him escape. Their hopes, their ideas, were all he had left. Chloe might be lying injured, not too far away. His first task was to find her.

He had an idea. Crawling backwards on his hands and knees, he slowly returned to the skeletons he and Chloe had found before. The gun the dead men had left behind was useless, but they might have other stuff—a torch, even.

Holding his breath, he felt around among the rags and bones until he found some belongings. A wallet. A scattering of change. *A box of matches.* Theo struck a light. A heady smell filled his nostrils as the match ignited and dazzled his eyes. Now he crept forwards again to the edge of the shaft. He stared into it.

*My only real friend is down there*, he thought. *I have to find out what happened to her. That's all that matters.*

He looked around, pondering his next move. Then he stopped, astonished. Somebody was waving at him. He blinked and looked again. There, some way down the tunnel, was the face of a kind old lady smiling at him. Her friendly features seemed to be caught in a beam of soft light. From the shadows the woman beckoned him, raising a single bright finger.

Spellbound, Theo began to walk forward. Just in time he remembered the shaft and stopped himself with a jolt. He swayed on the edge of the drop, about to plunge in, but somehow made a desperate leap to clear the distance.

He landed safely on the other side. The kindly face had disappeared. Theo let out a sigh of relief. It was short lived. Now he could hear footsteps. Not faint, creepy, ghostly footsteps, but bold, confident, striding ones. They were approaching from around the corner up ahead. Theo waited in the darkness, his heart pounding.

A policeman turned the corner. Not a modern-day policeman, but an old-fashioned constable, such as Theo had seen in his *Pictorial Tour of Victorian London*. The policeman's uniform was outdated, bulky, and brass-buttoned, with no holsters and flaps for radios and guns. The officer even wore huge side-whiskers, which were quite out of fashion nowadays—even Theo knew that.

The figure stopped on the corner and stood there, looking up and down the tunnel as if on duty. *I shouldn't be able to see that person*, Theo thought. *There's no light down here*. As with the kindly face, the visitor seemed to be illuminated by its own inner glow.

"Evening," the figure said.

*Is he talking to me?* Theo wondered. *Please don't let him be talking to me.* Theo stayed where he was, not daring to breathe.

"No cause for alarm, sir," the officer said, rocking slightly on his heels. "Just a routine patrol."

Theo remained silent. No book of manners could prepare him for an encounter like this.

"You can step out of the shadows, young feller," the constable said in a pleasant voice. "I know you're there! I realize the official uniform can be a bit imposing, but I don't bite, I can assure you!"

Theo took a deep breath and stepped nearer. There was no escape from the steady gaze of the constable, who appeared to be about fifty years old, craggy-faced, and robust.

"Can I help you in any way, sir?" the man asked.

Theo took a gamble. "I, um . . . seem to be a bit lost," he said. "Could you, err . . . tell me the way out?"

"Out?" the constable echoed. The word seemed to trouble him. "Out? I don't know what you mean, sir. . . ."

Theo stared at the figure. The policeman seemed to be losing his balance; his body quivered strangely.

"Very sorry, sir," the man said. "It's been a long time — I sometimes have trouble . . . remembering."

A pang of pity struck Theo, though he didn't know why.

"Remembering what?" he asked.

The constable stared sadly at him. "Remembering what I'm supposed to look like!" slurred an inhuman voice. Before Theo's eyes, the policeman began to fall apart. His body became transparent, and his skin peeled away on all sides — like a human banana — and slid to the floor with a hissing *flop*. For a second, a bright skeleton gaped at Theo before tumbling down, broken, into the molten slurry of the body.

Theo was forced to step over the terrifying remains, which were now slithering across the tunnel floor like a living pool. He fled blindly into the blackness. He crashed into a wall and slumped against it, panting.

"A visitor!" declared a ringing voice from behind him. Theo turned, trembling, to see a beautiful woman standing there. Like the other members of the Eighty-eight he had witnessed, she shone with her own inner radiance, which made her quite dazzling. Her sweeping, perfectly styled hair was white, and she wore a long, shimmering silver gown.

"How nice of you to drop by!" she continued, her voice sweet and cooing. "Except . . ."

Theo staggered backwards. "E-except . . . ?" he stammered.

"Visitors aren't allowed!" shrieked the woman, her jaw suddenly dropping and displaying a mouthful of razor-sharp teeth.

He turned and ran, reckless of any peril ahead. He feared the worst, expecting to be horribly killed at any instant. He tore through the darkness, away from the terrifying figures, every step bringing him hope of escape.

"Grab him!" a voice screamed, and Theo was clutched by clinging hands. But these weren't ghostly hands—they were warm flesh. And they dragged him through a hatch to safety. And the voices shouting his name were wonderfully familiar.

CHAPTER 20

# IN WHICH MYSTERIES ARE RESPECTED

HEO SANK INTO A COMFORTABLE pile of rugs and gazed with astonishment at Sam, Magnus, and a shame-faced but grinning Chloe.

"There!" said Sam. "Pretty blooming vigilant, I'd say."

"Unrelenting," smiled Magnus, tears leaking from his pale old eyes.

"Take it easy, Theo," said Chloe. "You're safe here for a while."

He took in his new surroundings. They seemed to be in a kind of narrow lumber room containing a crazy assortment of bric-a-brac, old books, diving equipment, a stuffed eagle, a rack of clothing, and an elephant gun. Electric strip lighting provided a pleasant glow. It seemed forever since Theo had felt safe and warm. He was so relieved to be back among friends.

Magnus had already retired to the far end of the room, to sit down in a big swivel chair before a bank of black-and-white viewing screens.

"He's never off duty," said Sam, smiling.

"How—how did you . . . ?" Theo had so many questions he didn't know where to start.

"When we fled from the Watchtower, Chloe told us to run to the safest place we know," Sam said. "Magnus dragged me down here, into the depths of the network."

"What is this place?"

"This is the bunker," Magnus piped up from the corner. "Set up a few years back by the Society as a kind of—*urrgh*—" He ran out of breath and sat gasping to himself.

"Better leave him," Sam said. "Too much excitement at once." He scuttled over into a corner and lit a gas ring. "All the modern conveniences," he added, pouring a bottle of liquid coffee essence into a pan. "Dunno how old this stuff is." He smiled. "They didn't do expiration dates in them days."

"You're supposed to dilute that muck," Chloe said to Sam. He ignored her.

Theo sighed and lay back. Now that he could relax for the first time in ages, a great wave of tiredness hit him. He could even feel his hands trembling. Chloe took a perch on a box nearby. Theo had a moment of double vision, for an instant seeing two Chloes. He shook his head to pull his wits together.

"I knew you'd be all right." Theo smiled up at Chloe. He felt almost tearful at seeing her again, but he did his best to cover it up.

"I got careless," Chloe said, tenderly feeling a bruise on the back of her head. Theo realized she had lost her peaked cap and found it strange to see her familiar shrewd face framed by a shock of dark brown hair.

"I stepped into a shaft," she said ruefully. "Slid down it and whacked my silly head at the bottom."

"We picked her up on the monitors!" Sam said. "We've had a vigilance camera system set up in the network for years. Haven't really had much reason to use it before. We'd spotted you both about an hour ago—snooping around. So we were on the alert, ready to pounce."

Chloe shook her head in disbelief. "You have this monitor station hidden in the heart of the network, and you didn't even tell me?"

"It's very clever," Sam said. "Norrowmore set it

up years ago, apparently. Tiny cameras hidden in the fungus globes. The enemy have never found them because the globes never need maintenance — each one is a little ecosystem."

"Neat. So you were spying on the enemy and up we popped instead!"

"Yes." Sam smiled. "We lost you for a bit when you ducked into the gulag. That maneuver even took Grandad by surprise. But as soon as Chloe fell down the shaft we spotted her again. Then we used a secret passageway to get close to Theo." He grinned. Sam offered Theo a mug of black coffee.

Theo accepted it, figuring it couldn't be much more dangerous than a ghostly policeman, an army of trigger-happy Foundlings, or a horde of smoglodytes.

Magnus plugged a mysterious little brown bottle up his nose and inhaled deeply. Sam passed the old man some coffee and two little white pills. The cemetery keeper swallowed the lot in one gulp, his Adam's apple bobbing crazily in his scrawny throat.

"It must seem a strange hideaway to you young ones," Magnus said in his feeble, wheezing voice. "So close to our enemies. But remember, the network had been quiet for decades till recently. None of the old combatants had much business here. It's only in the last couple of days we've had all this activity."

"Yeah—it's like an ants' nest now," said Sam.

"But," interrupted Theo, "don't you care how close you are to those—those ghosts?"

Magnus smiled. "No. I do not fear their presence myself, because I know what they are," he said, then fell silent.

"You can't just stop there!" shouted Theo. "What are they? There was a ghostly policeman and—other things," he said, not wishing to relive his experience quite yet.

"Now is not the time," Magnus said. "Chloe, I'd better have your full report."

Showing no signs of fatigue, Chloe sprang up and went to join Magnus at the monitor station.

"Not the time!" groaned Theo. "When I've just been attacked by them! What *would* he call a good time, then?"

Sam smiled. "Grandad's always like that. It's nice for me to see someone else get the treatment."

Theo did not look amused.

Sam drew him aside. "You must be starving," he said, showing Theo an enormous gray wall cupboard. Sam slid back a wooden door. "We're set up to withstand a long siege. Look at the supplies they've got here."

Theo, weak with hunger, studied the shelves of canned food. *Ox tongue, Eel in jelly. Condensed spinach.*

"Is it safe?" he asked.

"Course it is. Canned food can last for a hundred years," said Sam. "Reckon they must have stocked up just after World War Two." He picked up a rusting can. "Look at this one: *Ballast! The Ministry of Food's All-Purpose Root Vegetable Paste. See government instruction manual.*" Sam laughed. "Lucky we don't eat this rubbish today." Then he suddenly stopped grinning. "Well, actually we still do, because it's all there is!"

The two teenagers chuckled as they prepared the semblance of a hot supper for everyone. Theo had never had to look after himself before, and he made a horrible mess of the simplest culinary tasks, to Sam's amusement.

From the corner, Chloe watched and nudged Magnus. The old man's eyes sparkled.

"And you say," the old man whispered, "that he used his power—in front of your eyes?"

"Oh, yes," Chloe replied. "Once seen, never forgotten."

Magnus was sitting up now, with a new eagerness. "Against a foe? On purpose?"

"Yes — he saved my life, in fact."

Theo couldn't help overhearing this debate, as Magnus was a trifle deaf. The reminder that Theo had already proved useful enough to save Chloe from harm gave him a wonderful feeling inside. He looked around the cluttered bunker — at the new friends who all knew his name, asked him questions, needed his help. For a moment, among all the terror and dismay, life had a fleeting glow of perfection.

Magnus smiled at Chloe, his deep wrinkles softening as his whole being seemed to relax.

"All the requirements are satisfied," he whispered, still loud enough for Theo to hear. "I do believe it is time." He nodded profoundly, to no one in particular, then scurried off to hunt for something among the boxes.

After their meal, Magnus called for an end to the group's chatter, and hauled a battered leather case out from under an enormous old Union Jack.

"Theo Wickland," he said. "Please rise."

Theo looked across to Chloe, who shrugged. Theo rose, though his every bone requested otherwise.

"Since we freed you from Empire Hall," Magnus said, "we have been at war — fighting a diabolical foe who has given us little time to conduct our affairs as we would like."

"Hear hear!" shouted Sam. Magnus scowled at him.

"Winston Churchill!" Chloe grinned. "I like it!" But she shut up when she noticed that Magnus was looking sad.

"If things had been different—if Mr. Norrowmore hadn't died—if we had been able to contact the Council, then things would have been done properly. There were plans, Theo, to educate you gently into the special role, unique to the Wickland family, that you are destined to assume."

Magnus dropped his grand orator style, to rest against the back of a chair and take a breather. "We didn't want to frighten you, lad," he confessed with a disarming smile, "by telling you too much all at once. But now, as it often turns out in wartime, we don't have the luxury of doing things right. We just have to get on and do them."

Theo felt a tingle running up his spine. But he also felt anxious. Mysteries and destinies were great when they were off somewhere in the distance, not when they actually became true in front of your eyes.

Magnus opened the suitcase. He pulled out an enormous black cape and draped it over Theo's

shoulders. Then he reached inside the box and produced a pair of black leather gauntlets. He motioned
to Theo to try them on.

"The Ascendancy is upon us," Magnus said. "A
scion of the House of Wickland, on the brink of adult-
hood, has shown the special powers. At last, after a
hundred years, London has a new Candle Man."

Theo felt faint. *So that was the Ascendancy*, he
thought to himself. *It was me all along!* Suddenly his
fatigue finally hit him. The room swam before his
eyes.

"You'll look a right fool in that lot," he heard Chloe
say—then he passed out.

---

Chloe was leaving. This had been decided while
Theo was asleep. Obviously becoming a legendary
hero didn't yet entitle him to join in any important
decision-making.

"You're okay, Theo—just exhausted," Chloe said,
loading up her backpack. "It'll be safer for you to
stay here for the next few hours."

"What are you going to do?" Theo was feeling
better again now and tucking into a tin of cabbage
for breakfast.

"While you were asleep," Chloe said, "Magnus

and I looked at the laptop Foley stole from Dr. Saint. There's enough evidence on there for the police to move in on him and shut down his so-called charity. I've got to get it to Sergeant Crane."

Theo's heart sank. "Can't we all go?" he asked. "I think it'll be a big mistake to split up!"

Chloe sat down next to him and spoke gently. "Don't worry about me, Theo. I know what I'm doing! The enemy has been sealing up the exits to the network, but one person who knows it well enough could still get out."

"I don't like it," Theo said. He had only just been reunited with Chloe. He felt safer, stronger, with her around. He didn't want to lose her again.

"It's our best hope," Chloe insisted, trying to look cheerful. "If I can get Crane to authorize a search of the network, we'll have an army of officers—enough to drive out the Society of Good Works and stop whatever they're up to."

Theo still looked doubtful.

Chloe rose and pulled on her coat. "Once I've handed the evidence to Crane or Finley, I'll get some reinforcements and come back for you guys."

"It's too dangerous out there!" Theo protested. "You've got the smoglodytes, Foundlings—and the Dodo after you."

Chloe smiled. "Don't be daft, Theo. It's not *me* they want—they're all after you!"

"Terrific. Now I feel a lot better," Theo said, moping.

"It's perfect!" Sam said with forced enthusiasm. Theo guessed that Sam didn't want to lose Chloe either. "We can just sit tight here and Chloe will mobilize the forces of law and order. Bingo!"

"It just doesn't feel right. The 'forces of law and order' don't seem to have helped much in this weird war so far," Theo said. "If I have these powers, maybe I should be using them," he added.

They all fell silent.

"Fair point," chirped Sam.

Magnus nodded sagely. "If the Candle Man is against the idea, then we really must listen to him. The Wicklands have a special instinct in these matters!"

"Rot!" said Chloe, selecting a new hat from the piles of gear in the bunker. She chose a khaki military policeman's cap. "What else can we do? What's your plan B?"

This question was answered by a long silence. Chloe pulled on her backpack and got ready to leave.

Theo jumped up, dismayed. "We can stay together, spy on them—" he began.

Chloe shook her head. "Then what? Defeat an army of fanatics and monsters with an old man and two drippy teenage boys? Sorry, gang, but it's up to me. Luckily, I'm the cool heroic type."

Chloe opened the hatch and was gone.

# CHAPTER 21

# A MISTAKE

TRISTUS SOARED ACROSS THE London skies, thick yellow fog blotting his presence out from human eyes. The battle against the smoglodytes had left him weak; their foul toxins still clouded his mind and sapped his strength. But at last he felt strong enough to return to the fray—or what was left of it, depending on how long he had been out of action.

*Watch the boy*, Norrowmore had told him. *If necessary, help with the escape.* Norrowmore had said that Tristus could feel absolved after that. He could go away and dream his stone dream forever, forget the humans, the war, everything. But that had been months ago. What had happened to Norrowmore now, and his endless delicate machinations to free the boy?

*Something is wrong.* Tristus swooped low over the Condemned Cemetery, the great field of bones and stone images where he could blend in so perfectly. Its quiet walks of memory were not as he had left them. The cottage where the cemetery keeper lived was smashed and deserted. Tristus snarled, revealing fangs he seldom showed the world. The cottage had been one of Norrowmore's planned refuges for the boy. The garghoul sensed enemy action.

He flew swiftly to the cemetery wall and scanned the windows of Empire Hall with his bright, penetrating eyes.

Something had changed. Lights shone in every window, figures strode the corridors with arrogant steps, a dangerous aura of energy crackled in the air. The Society of Good Works was in rude health, showing evidence of power and confidence that even Norrowmore had little suspected.

Tristus knew he had to speak to his old friend. The great design was not working out as planned. Norrowmore had always insisted that they meet rarely, for purposes of secrecy, but this was an emergency. The garghoul flew over the smog-bound city, a gray blur in the murky night. He soon reached his destination.

The elegant dome of the Watchtower was shattered. Blackened beams jutted up like burnt ribs. Gone was the soft bleep of electronic signals, the quiet, endless chatter of human communications. Instead there were ashes, the smell of outdoors, of rain and ruin.

It didn't take long for the garghoul to dig out the skull of his dead friend. He held the charred shell in his rough hands, studying it with a pang of wonder. There was something else here too—lingering traces of a substance, a subtle poison that had finally ended the life of the old man.

His keen senses alerted, Tristus now detected another odor as well, an acrid vapor creeping up through the Watchtower. It was the smell of alchemy. The rank, dangerous scent took him back to a place and a time he had hoped to forget forever. His usually passive face twisted into a grimace of anguish as the memories hit home.

It was the last place he wanted to go, but there was little choice. *This war is not over*, he told himself. The bony hand of Norrowmore seemed to be pointing the way.

---

"Dead?" asked Lady Blessing.

"Yes, shot dead by one of the Outer Network Patrols," said Baron Patience. He cut a ridiculous figure leading the twelve-strong work party along the flooded tunnel in his best salmon-fishing waders. There wasn't much that could bring a smile to his face, but for once he enjoyed a self-satisfied smirk.

"It looks like our fortunes are changing. The Vessel led us on a right goose chase for a while, but now he's out of the picture. And it looks like this new killing has turned out to be rather a spot of luck."

Lady Blessing motioned to the party to stop. They had reached the final bend in the tunnels before their destination. With her black hooded cloak on, the natural pallor of her angular face made her look like an elegant phantom.

"Luck? In what way?"

"Oh, we've eliminated a very significant member of the Vigilance apparently—a young lady. Dr. Saint has asked to see the body. The funny thing is, the guard—hopeless bungler—didn't even mean to kill her. He saw her in one of the tunnels near the surface, and only meant to scare her with a warning shot, he says."

"How kind of him!" Lady Blessing exclaimed. "A most considerate gesture that went wrong. He must be terribly upset!"

"Awfully. In fact, I heard him and the other guards having a big laugh over it—to conceal their true feelings."

"Stout lads," said Lady Blessing.

"It really is the kind of happy accident that makes one feel destiny is on our side. The time is ripe for our Good Works to spread out across this once-great Empire!" declared the Baron.

The heavy equipment had now arrived. Lady Blessing studied a chart and addressed the troop of Foundling engineers. "Circle three, junction fourteen-A. One of the last hatches on this level to be sealed. It's a type C—late Victorian. Don't damage the percussive membrane. After this, we can all proceed—"

"I—I thought I saw something!" blurted out Baron Patience.

"Just a rat, of course!" snapped Lady Blessing. "Honestly! Now, come on men, as fast as you can—this stinking sewer is ruining my best boots." The engineers stepped into the branch tunnel, dragging their torches and gas cylinders through the black waters.

"Look! Another rat. Monster of a beast!" gasped the Baron, pointing at the huge bedraggled creature huddled on the hatch cover. It let out a hideous squeal. One of the men threw a wrench at it but missed. The rodent slipped away into the shadows.

There was a scream. An engineer was suddenly dragged down under the black waters. Baron Patience gaped. The thick coils of a monstrous snake were glimpsed momentarily in the bubbling slime. The engineer thrashed around horribly, then was gone.

"Out! Get out!" shrieked Lady Blessing, racing away down the tunnel. She stopped dead. A dark shape barred her way. A caped figure with an enormous hooked nose and stiff, clawlike hands confronted her.

"You dare!" rumbled a deep, terrifying voice. "You have the nerve to come here and seal off my ancient right of access to the network?"

"The Dodo!" cried Lady Blessing.

Baron Patience clutched at his chest, as if fearing imminent heart failure. "We—we meant no harm!" he stammered. "Call off your creatures! I assure you, we—" The Baron's explanation was brought to a premature halt, as he was dragged away by a dripping tentacle. "Noooo!"

The Dodo snorted. "Obnoxious fellow," he said.

Lady Blessing couldn't resist a quick peep at the Baron's demise.

"By all means, kill the others," she said brightly, affecting a girlish enthusiasm for the idea. "But you must protect *me*—preserve one eloquent voice to express your . . . your justified outrage to Dr. Saint."

"A noble thought," said the Dodo, while screams filled the tunnel around them. "But my servants may not want any of you filth to get away."

"I—I can tell you things you need to know!" Lady Blessing gabbled. "Everything's changed. You'll want to join the Society now—we hold all the cards."

A strange calm had now resumed. A quick glance revealed to Lady Blessing that only she and the Dodo were left standing in the tunnel.

"Indeed," growled the Dodo. "And what has changed?"

"For one thing," she said with a cold smile, "the Vessel is dead. In fact, there is a *new* Candle Man," she added teasingly. She studied the Dodo's heavy-lidded eyes for a reaction, but they remained veiled, distant.

The Dodo threw back his enormous head and let out a high-pitched whistle. Moments later, a tiny gray bat flapped gently down from the shadows above and clung tamely to the Dodo's withered hand. Lady Blessing watched wide-eyed as the grotesque figure exchanged an outlandish shrill dialogue with the little bat.

"Wickland dead?" the Dodo retorted. "*We* don't think so." Lady Blessing's pale face went even whiter as the hulking figure lurched towards her. "You see? I believe I have more reliable sources of information than the lying tongue of a Society witch," he said, stroking the fur of the bat's head with infinite gentleness.

Hatchway C/14A opened behind Lady Blessing and two men in white coats and goggles stepped out.

Lady Blessing threw back her dark hood and shook out her long raven hair proudly. "I'm too beautiful to die," she said through gritted teeth. "I know I could be very useful to you." She forced a rather ugly, desperate smile.

The Dodo stopped to ponder for a moment.

"Maybe you're right," he replied. "Take her away. I could use someone to muck out the mammoth."

The Dodo let out a sudden series of barks. From the other side of the hatch an excited stamping of hooves was heard in reply. Lady Blessing watched in silence as a horde of creatures she had never seen before in her life began to pour into the tunnel.

"Now I have an appointment with young Mr. Wickland," murmured the Dodo. "An appointment from which only one of us will emerge alive."

# CHAPTER 22

# DISCOVERY

*B*OOM. EVERYTHING CHANGED AFTER Chloe left. The gloomy silence of the network's eternal night was broken—by shuddering surges of power. The three remaining members of the Society of Unrelenting Vigilance gathered around the old monitors, their faces lit by the silvery radiance of the screens. There was no sign of Chloe—or any other human activity.

"She must have touched something!" Sam wailed. "She's set off an alarm!"

The explosions of power rumbled on in a regular, thundering cycle. The temperature was rising. The bunker already felt like a tropical hothouse.

"I told you coming down here was a rotten idea!" Sam complained, wiping his sweaty face on his grimy shirt. "There's stuff going on in the network that we don't know about! We've got to get out!"

"We are safe in here," said Magnus, who had taken off his tatty old raincoat and now sat in a threadbare white vest.

"But it's getting too hot to handle, isn't it?" nagged Sam. "Oh, yes. Chloe knew this was going to happen!" Theo and Magnus gave Sam a dark look. Sam sat down on a crate biting his nails like a worried child.

Theo wondered how much older Sam was than he—only a year at most, he guessed. They could almost have been schoolmates—if Dr. Saint had ever let him go to school and have funny friends like Sam.

"Don't worry," said Theo. He didn't like to see Sam like this. It made his own worries seem all the more real. He wanted to pat Sam on the back reassuringly, as Chloe often did, but he couldn't work out how hard or where to hit him.

"What is there *not* to worry about?" Sam moaned.

*Throom.* The booming noise became louder. Sam grabbed a pack of bottled water and ripped the plastic cover off with nervous energy. He passed drinks round to the others as if administering relief at a disaster.

"We might be *hidden* here," Sam said, "but we could still get cooked alive."

Theo pulled off his jacket and sat there in a gray T-shirt he had borrowed from Chloe. Sweat was starting to run down his back. They sat in anxious silence as the network creaked and groaned around them.

"I just wish I knew what they were up to!" Sam moaned.

Theo pondered. He had been developing a theory. It was time, he decided, for the Candle Man to solve a mystery. He didn't know much about being a hero, but he did know it didn't involve being a complete waste of space.

"I wasn't allowed to read newspapers or history books when I was at Empire Hall," Theo began, swigging his lukewarm water. "They wanted me to be ignorant of the real world."

"Not quite the time for your life story!" groaned Sam.

Theo grinned. A couple of days with Chloe had prepared him for that kind of attitude. "But," Theo continued, "Mr. Nicely thought it would be funny to let me read *boring* things: plans, maps, blueprints, and so on. Like he'd give me a diagram of a sewage works to look at for the evening."

"Your life sounds more exciting than mine!" grumbled Sam.

"When Chloe first showed me Foley's secret map of the whole network, she asked me what I thought it was. Then she laughed at my answer."

"Why?" Sam asked. "What did you tell her?"

"I said it was some sort of machine," said Theo. There was a pause, broken by the distant screeching of vapor in tubes. "I think all the tunnels, vaults, and canals add up to make one big device."

Sam's eyes grew bigger. "This is supposed to make me feel better, is it?" He gulped.

"But think about it," said Theo. "The Society of Good Works is down here in force. They're hardly likely to do anything to endanger themselves, are they?"

"Look," said Magnus suddenly. "Everyone's leaving!"

Sam and Theo jumped up and joined Magnus at the Vigil Station. Screens that had previously shown no action at all now revealed figures climbing stairways, long lines of people walking towards exit hatchways. It was an exodus, a calm, orderly evacuation.

"It's like they're abandoning ship," murmured Magnus.

"Leaving us trapped like rats!" groaned Sam.

"Not all of them are leaving," Magnus said. "One or two people—Dr. Saint, in particular—cannot be accounted for. Now look here," he croaked, pointing with a knotty finger at a fuzzy screen. "It shows a glimpse of the tunnel leading to the center of enemy operations. That is our target—" Magnus was about to say more, when a yelp from Sam cut him short.

"What is that?" gasped Sam. He was no longer staring at the screens but towards the corner of the ceiling. Dark slime seemed to be oozing down through a crack.

"There's more!" Theo said, pointing to black bubbles that seemed to have grown through tiny gaps in the ceiling and were now swelling like balloons. Even Magnus got up from his chair, grabbed a walking stick, and staggered across to get a closer look. One of the black shapes fell to the floor with a *flop*.

"Stand back!" Magnus cried. "They've found us!"

Skun, chief tracker of the smoglodyte tribe, reared up from the floor. Grinning like a little gray imp, he wobbled from side to side as his innards rearranged themselves into the right places.

"I can see you!" Skun cooed in a singsong voice, his narrow little eyes squinting towards Theo. Skun was ecstatic. Truly he was the greatest tracker of all. He had now found the precious Theo *twice*. This time, nothing would go wrong. Another black blob squelched to the floor and began to re-form itself.

"A very clever hidey-hole!" Skun said. "But I've been hunting for you *so* long—and it's been *such* hard work . . ."

". . . and Dr. Saint has been so very cross with us . . . ," butted in the second intruder.

". . . that we just couldn't give up until we got you!" completed the third, sprouting up to join its companions.

*Three of them*, Theo thought, upset by the recurrence of his unfavorite number. *This is bad*.

Magnus reached for the enormous old blunderbuss, but the smoglodyte leader leapt through the air and kicked him to the floor.

"Naughty naughty!" Skun mocked, jumping up and down on the old man.

"Leave him alone!" shrieked Sam. He landed a punch on the smoglodyte tracker, sending Skun flying into the wall. But the creature simply bounced back like a rubber ball and landed on its feet, cackling.

"Plenty of time to get even with *you*," Skun hissed, his long tongue flickering out.

Sam didn't have much time to worry about this threat, as the second smoglodyte sprang on him from behind and wrapped its flexible body around Sam's head.

Theo rushed to help, but Skun's tiny foot snaked out and sent him sprawling across the floor. Theo picked himself up, angrily peeling off his leather gauntlets.

"Can't—can't breathe!" gasped Sam, as the smoglodyte squeezed itself tighter around his face and throat. Magnus was still lying, dazed, nearby.

"Stop!" Theo screamed at the top of his voice. "I'm—I'm warning you!" The smoglodyte wrapped around Sam's throat looked towards Theo. For a moment it seemed unsure. Then it resumed its fiendish grip.

"Nah," it said. "I'm having far too much fun."

*Pop.* It was the last thing the smog said. Theo reached out to grab it, but the moment his fingertips came into contact, it exploded into gray dust. Everyone in the room—including Theo—stared in astonishment as a fine rain of ash and stringy innards dropped to the ground.

"What—what happened?" stammered Skun,

backing away. Theo could see the smog's heart pumping with panic inside its skinny chest.

"Dunno!" squeaked the other. It had been creeping up on the fallen figure of Magnus and was now reaching for the old man's neck. Theo was so fired up by rage he leapt straight at it, grabbing it by the ankle before it could flit away. Moments later there *was* no ankle—the imp went *pop*, just like the other one had. Theo grimaced as the sticky wet guts hit him in the face.

In a desperate attempt to escape, Skun sprang towards the crack in the ceiling. Theo leapt to stop the fleeing smog and just managed to brush the creature with his fingertips.

Skun's skin bubbled, blistered, but did not explode. Squealing with pain, the wounded imp squeezed his body feebly through the crack, leaving a syrupy brown stain behind him. The smog attack had been turned into a rout.

"Yes!" cheered Sam, punching the air in a triumphant gesture. "We've got the Candle Man!" Then he sank to the ground again and knelt there, panting.

Theo helped Magnus to sit up.

"I knew I was right!" the old man wheezed. "The Ascendancy is vindicated! Well done, lad."

Theo bent down to examine a black streak of smog-bits smeared across the floor. "But what happened to them?" he asked. "How did I *do* it?"

Magnus mopped up some of the remains with a tissue and put them in a jar to study later.

"I believe," he said at last, "that smoglodytes—like the garghouls—are creatures from an earlier age of this earth. They are semi-solid beings of skin and gas. Almost impossible to destroy by physical force, but very sensitive to other forms of energy. The power in you, Theo, called *tripudon* by some—or *jump energy*—obviously makes them combust in some way."

The fact that there was a name for his power was of secondary concern to Theo in the wake of the attack.

"But are they . . . dead?" Theo asked.

"Don't worry—these ones can't harm us again! Whether they are destroyed forever, I don't know. Some reports say that smoglodytes can re-form themselves out of polluted air. But the process would take many years."

"What about that last one? I think it was wounded, but it got away."

Magnus frowned. "Who knows? But the fact is, we are discovered. Chloe's idea that we stay put is no longer an option."

"Good," said Sam. "Anyway, with Theo's powers we may get out of this yet!"

Theo wasn't so sure.

Magnus beckoned the others over to the Vigil Station.

"Get out of this?" he echoed. "I think we may do a little more than that," he said. "The screens are all telling the same story. The network has been sealed for a special purpose. Water levels inside are ris-ing—probably through a sluice connected to the Thames. In the main network, everyone is making their way to the surface!"

Magnus looked perplexed for a moment, as a dark shape, rather resembling a big cat, loped across one of the screens. He fiddled with the focus for a moment, then ignored it.

"That means—apart from rather a lot of stray creatures that seem to be trapped down here—the only ones left behind in the network will be us . . . and a few smoglodyte guards." There was a twinkle in his eye. Was it happiness, inspiration, or complete madness? Theo could not tell.

"And as Theo has just demonstrated, we have no need to fear them anymore." He grabbed the boys around the shoulders, supporting his skeletal frame between them.

"I think we can get through to Dr. Saint now," he said. "I believe we may yet stop him with just an old man and two boys. I actually think, my dear comrades, that after all these years, the Society of Unrelenting Vigilance is going to win!"

# CHAPTER 23

# DEEP WATERS

"I T WAS KIND OF YOU TO BRING me along, sir,"
said Mr. Nicely. He spoke as quietly as he could,
because otherwise the smoglodytes' ears pricked up
and they looked at him. "But I rather feel a squad of
muscle-bound Foundlings would have been more
help."

They were standing on the great garghoul monument at the bottom of the network. Dr. Saint, in a
stained and crumpled charcoal gray suit, watched
the smoglodytes as they busied themselves digging.

"I don't need mindless brawn, Mr. Nicely," Dr.
Saint said. "That's what I released this tribe of

villains for." He flashed his white teeth, but it wasn't the reassuring smile of old.

"I need someone who will walk beside me, behold my every action, smile at my every deed, and still report back to the world that I am a wonderful human being."

Mr. Nicely nodded, but it was difficult for him to get used to this new version of his employer. For a start, Dr. Saint's face had become inclined to drip; at the moment, the corner of his mouth was melting away, revealing rather more of tooth and gum than was usually acceptable in society.

"I need someone by me who will do exactly as I say, without question, because he is terrified of me," said Dr. Saint.

Mr. Nicely frowned, then swallowed hard.

"All, err . . . extreme kindness is rather awe-inspiring, sir," he said. "You *could* call it an element of fear," he conceded.

"Oh, drop it, man!" Dr. Saint sneered. "We don't have to act anymore — not in front of these vermin!"

Mr. Nicely looked away. All around them the industrious imps were scurrying, bending, and scraping. Mr. Nicely did his best to ignore what they were actually doing.

Dr. Saint strode down among the stone markers.

He climbed over a pile of freshly dug ashes and stared down into the ground at his feet. There, sprawled out in a shallow pit, a yard taller than the biggest man, was the enormous body of an uru-ghoul, the fearsome warrior class of garghoul.

Its eyes stared up blankly, yet there was a curious intensity about that sightless gaze, as if it could hold you and keep you spellbound for eternity. Its horns were glittering and sharp, like black diamonds. Its skin was shining and crystalline, as if chipped out of obsidian. The magnificent, terrible creature was but one of hundreds, each being unearthed from its own separate burial mound.

"He is impressive, is he not, my lord?" wheedled a small voice next to the doctor. It was Gank, the smoglodytes' tribal leader.

"Oh, yes." Dr. Saint sighed with studied noncha-lance. "The urughoul could rip a human being apart as if he were made of wet paper."

"And you—oh great Philanthropist—will wisely bring them back to life?" the little smog asked in a whining tone.

"That is the noble purpose of the Liberation," Dr. Saint replied coldly. "To release the poor, forgotten ones who were left down here, and give them Good Work to do."

"Yes," said Gank dejectedly. "They eat us," he added, looking up at Dr. Saint with a pitiful smile.

"I know," replied the doctor. He looked around to check he was not observed, then lay a hand gently on the smoglodyte's shoulder. He watched with satisfaction as Gank popped out of existence.

"Too much going on in the mind of that one," he remarked to nobody in particular. Satisfied with all he had seen, he headed back to the stairway, Mr. Nicely struggling to keep up in his galoshes.

———⚬✦⚬———

"Careful, Sam!" warned Magnus. "One false move and we're all done for!"

"Don't be such an old worry-guts," said Sam. "Theo's plans aren't *allowed* to go wrong!"

Getting out of the bunker had been trickier than expected. Water had risen up over the main entrance, so they had been forced to use an overhead hatchway. A narrow crawl space had brought them back to the required tunnel, but this was flooded too — with hot, foul, smoking water.

It had been Theo's idea to take a gigantic fungus globe apart and use the glass dome as a boat. Now that Sam had clambered aboard, the three of them were speeding down the flooded passageway with

220

ease, instead of having to wade and swim through poisonous waters.

"It's this Ascendancy thing," Sam babbled on. "Now that Theo's got his powers, he's a new man — a real hero! I'll bet there's a magic ring and stuff that goes with that costume of yours!"

Theo groaned. "I'm still the same me," Theo protested. "Just because Magnus dug out an old moth-eaten costume — "

"Which you are not wearing," Magnus observed.

Theo wiggled his fingers to show he had donned the vintage-edition Candle Man gloves. They were more supple than the cumbersome gauntlets Dr. Saint had made him wear. Those old gloves only reminded him of his miserable years of confinement anyway.

"I've borrowed Lord Wickland's gloves, but I haven't earned the right to be Candle Man yet. I'm no hero," Theo mumbled.

"It takes courage to admit that," said Magnus, huddled deep in the dome.

"*Heroic* courage," added Sam warmly.

Theo sighed. All these years the Society of Unrelenting Vigilance had wanted a new Candle Man to help them fight their foes. Now they were determined to have one — apparently whether Theo liked it or not.

"What's more, I am beginning to think Theo's theory is correct," Magnus murmured. His long frame was squeezed awkwardly in the boat, and his bony left elbow was jutting into Sam's soft stomach. Theo was in the stern, perched on Magnus's bulging backpack. "The Society has always assumed that the network is merely a subterranean highway used by secret groups to avoid the police and the attention of the unsuspecting populace above. *Hurrgh*."

"Hit him!" Sam shouted, and Theo did his best to whack Magnus in the small of his back and get his antique inner-workings back in line again.

"Honestly," Sam groaned. "How can anyone so short of breath be so long-winded?"

Magnus gasped and spluttered a bit, then carried on.

"But this 'machine' theory of yours, Master Wickland, is rather compelling!" The dome-boat struck some floating debris and became lodged against an archway.

"Now we're up the creek!" Sam said.

Theo, who was freer to move than the others, dragged a wooden post from the water, nearly tipping everyone out in the process. With all his strength he thrust the post against the wall and sent the inverted dome spinning elegantly back into the main current.

"Candle Man to the rescue," cheered Sam.

"Well, I suppose it's just like steering a coracle," Theo replied, pleased with himself. "Page two hundred and six, *Inland Waterway Navigation: A Visual Record*. I've often wanted to try riding in one."

"We are making excellent progress," Magnus said, peering ahead.

"Towards what?" Theo asked. In the dank, steaming gloom he could hardly see a thing.

"The center of things," Magnus replied. "Yes, it all adds up!" There was a spark in those sunken old eyes. "The original enemy of our Society, the Philanthropist, was an alchemist. It is well known that he performed some of his experiments down here. But it never occurred to me — or Mr. Norrowmore — that the entire network could be one single device."

Magnus dipped his fingers in the filmy waters and pulled them out sharply.

"Almost boiling!" he remarked. "These canals — obviously mixed with forbidden oils — complete the picture perfectly. Alchemists perform their dark miracles by combining earth, air, fire, and water in secret combinations."

Theo had to fend the dome away from the wall again as they were pushed to the side by more and more floating debris.

"The water," Magnus theorized, "well, we're sailing on that now. The air, of course, we are breathing. The earth—minerals—I believe are in the chemicals that Theo and Chloe saw the Society pouring into the canals last night."

"And the fire?" Theo asked. But he had a horrible feeling he knew the answer already.

That was when they crashed. The dome smashed into a sluice gate and hurled the three of them into the midst of a smoglodyte guard post.

———◆———

*My deeds will go down in smoglodyte history*, Skun reflected as he crawled upside down along the tunnel roof, towards the Inner Sentry Station. This guarded the way up to the Well Chamber—where Dr. Saint was.

Given the almost impossible task of tracking one lost boy in a London that had swollen to dizzying size, he had found Theo twice. This time, the boy was right here, in the network. All he had to do was explain his mission to the guards, then report directly to Dr. Saint. At last his task would be over, his fame assured.

"I'm back," he cried out, dropping lightly to the floor. He grimaced as the landing hurt his shriveled

224

leg. "Skun—the hero!" He winced bravely.

The other smogs gathered round him eagerly. "What's the news, Skun? What have you done?"

Skun took a deep breath—but suddenly everything happened at once.

"Attack! We're under attack!" screeched a voice through the mists. From over by the sluice gate, the smoglodyte guards had started screaming. There was a series of explosions and they screamed no more.

They had been caught completely by surprise. The enemy had penetrated almost to the Well Chamber by cunning use of the canal system. In a brilliant attack they had launched three desperate agents from a fast-moving craft that had smashed into the sluice gate under the cover of the hot mists.

"Human scum!" shrieked Lurk, a wrinkly old smog. The battle was drawing closer. Skun could already see figures darting here and there through the vapors. He ducked to avoid the flying bits as someone he vaguely knew burst into a ball of gas and giblets.

"There's three of them!" Lurk screamed. "And they've got a special weapon!"

*Three* of them, Skun realized with a sinking heart. It was *them*. The humans were trying to escape him again!

"Get back!" he cried to his tribesmen. He couldn't believe his rotten smoglodyte luck.

"It's the Candlehand!" old Lurk suddenly wailed. "The hour of doom is nigh!"

Skun shrank into a crevice in the rock. The Candlehand? Was that the answer? Was that why his triumphant hunt had ended in such disaster? Was the boy they had been seeking really their most terrifying myth come back to life?

"Back to the Well Chamber!" Skun cried, leaping towards the stairway. But his injury slowed him down. "We must warn the masters!"

*Crack.* A blast of buckshot pierced his hide, and he flew out of control like a deflating balloon and slapped into the stone wall.

"But we don't want you warning *anyone*," croaked a tall, ancient human, stepping forwards and lowering an enormous gun.

———◦•◦———

"They've retreated!" Magnus shouted. Theo glanced around nervously, his hands still glowing. Being hurled out of the dome had shaken him up a bit, but he was determined no harm would come to his friends. Now he watched with relief as the remaining smoglodytes scattered in the gloom.

"They've returned to the — *hurrghh* — foul elements that spawned them!" Magnus crowed. Then, flushed with triumph, the cemetery keeper leant on the blunderbuss, laughing and gasping for breath at the same time.

*Completely mad*, thought Theo. He frowned at Sam, who was dancing some kind of jig.

"We did it!" Sam said. "We won!"

"Just like the old days!" said Magnus, reloading the gun with trembling fingers.

Theo was not celebrating. He felt afraid. Every victory took him closer to an encounter with Dr. Saint, the man who had lied to him, imprisoned him, controlled him all his life. Hundreds of people were at his command — supernatural creatures did his bidding, and he had the power to influence the police and the government. How could you beat a man like that?

Then there was Mr. Nicely. The so-called best friend who had laughed and grinned and twirled his umbrella while Theo's life was wasted, strangled, betrayed every single day of his existence. Would Theo's hands glow when the jolly-faced butler came into view? Could Theo use his powers against the only people he had ever really known?

Magnus had reloaded his museum-piece and

handed the backpack to Sam. They walked ahead, side by side, through the abandoned sentry post, towards Dr. Saint's secret center of operations.

"This is it," Magnus whispered. "The reason we've been vigilant all these years. To stop the enemy returning and winning the war. To restore the Candle Man, so there will always be a light to dispel the darkness of the underworld."

Theo had hardly been paying attention. He followed them like a sleepwalker. He was listening to the distant booms, the surging of vapors in hidden pipes, the seething of energy that echoed all around them. He suddenly knew what it reminded him of.

*The network*, he told himself, *is a giant Mercy Tube.*

CHAPTER **24**

# THE WELL CHAMBER

IT WAS BEYOND ANYTHING THEY HAD expected. They emerged from the tunnel onto an iron platform that ran all the way round an enormous circular chamber. In the middle was a dark tower, rising from a gulf of mists like a mountainous stalagmite. Bright lights glittered at its peak. Four narrow iron bridges linked the tower to the surrounding chamber, and below them was a drop that seemed to go down forever.

"Your monitors never showed us this," Sam breathed.

"No," confessed Magnus, his eyes streaming with tears from the stinging vapors. "We never got a spy

229

camera in here. It's the Philanthropist's old center of operations. Legend calls this place the Well Chamber. We are the first Vigilance agents ever to set foot in here—*hurrgh*." Magnus paused to gasp for breath. "It looks like the evacuation has left it almost deserted—except for whoever is in the control tower at the top."

"Look," Theo said, his keen eyes picking out a fragile framework that rose from the top of the tower and disappeared into the darkness overhead. "Some sort of Otis shaft."

"Normal people call them elevators," said Sam.

"I've never seen an elevator before," Theo replied, "or a normal person, for that matter."

"It would appear," Magnus said, "that Dr. Saint has his own express elevator into the heart of this place."

"Yeah—and out of it," noted Sam. Behind them, the rising waters had churned up through the tunnel and were now spilling over the platform, threatening to wash the three of them over the edge.

"We've got to move," Magnus said. "Dangerous or not, that tower is now the safest place to be! To the bridge!" he cried, his walking stick skidding on the slippery iron surface.

Sam was about to step onto the bridge when he

was hit by a flying black blur. A final smoglodyte guard, hidden by the vapors, sprang straight at his throat, its spidery hands seeking a death hold on the soft flesh. But it was the smoglodyte that didn't have a chance. Theo reached out and exploded the astonished creature with one swift touch. A small, foul drizzle spattered Sam, and a little dark cloud spread out across the paler mists of the chamber.

"Yuck," said Sam, smearing the smog-stains off his cheek and onto his shirt. "Thanks for the save, Candle Man!"

Theo avoided Sam's gaze as he stepped onto the narrow bridge, still awkward at the faint hint of hero worship. But he couldn't deny he felt different now. He wasn't just a bewildered escapee—as he had been at first—or a generally useless passenger, as he had felt with Chloe. Now he was part of a team and—looking at the sagging, bony Magnus and the red-faced, anxious Sam—he began to feel like he might have to emerge as the leader.

They continued the crossing in silence. Clouds rose from the depths below and drifted around them like enormous phantoms. Theo hoped that the very vapors created by Dr. Saint would be his undoing, enabling a small group of determined enemies to creep into the heart of operations unseen.

Suddenly an ear-splitting *bang* made them all jump.

"What was that?" Sam yelped.

*Bang, bang*—all around the chamber, the jarring sounds rang out. The trio froze, uncertain. Then the bridge began to tremble. Suddenly they heard a rapid *clack, clack, clack*—as if an invisible train were approaching.

"Move!" Magnus shouted. "That way!" He pointed towards the tower.

Theo glanced backwards to see a shocking sight. The metal bridge was retracting. It no longer reached the platform behind them. It had been automatically released and was being reeled in. *Clack, clack, clack*—the gray slats vanished into each other.

"Faster!" Theo cried, as they raced towards the control tower, the bridge disappearing under their feet. He didn't dare glance back—or down.

"Go!" With a desperate cry, Sam actually shoved his grandad over the last few yards, leaving himself and Theo to make a wild leap for the tower.

"Made it!" Sam gasped. They had landed in a heap on an iron balcony, just as the last slats of the bridge rattled into the wall. They crouched in the dark, listening for any sounds of alarm.

"It would seem the retraction of the bridge was

automatic," Magnus wheezed, sitting up and trying to recover his dignity. The bulging veins in his neck and forehead were pulsing as if ready to burst. "I don't think anyone in the tower has spotted us." They kept to the shadows, looking to the right and left, but no guards appeared.

"It seems their plans hold all their attention," Magnus said. He nodded upwards, where lights were blinking and the whirring of machines could be heard. A metal staircase led up from the balcony, inviting them to make the final ascent. Magnus gave his blunderbuss to Sam and grabbed the ladder with both gnarled hands.

Theo peeled his gloves off and looped the gauntlets over his belt. His hands were glowing—that meant at least one murderer was nearby. Exhausted in every muscle, he followed the others up.

They clambered to the top of an abandoned observation post. From there, they could look down on the main platform, from which Dr. Saint appeared to be controlling operations. The three crouched behind an iron barrier and caught their breath.

Sam nudged Theo forwards to take a peek, as he was the "luckiest." Peering around the barrier, at first Theo could make out nothing, but soon the fitful mists dispersed enough to reveal the scene.

In the center of the platform was the main control station—a semicircular array of great iron wheels, valves, and levers—all under a metal storm-hood to protect it from the very forces it could unleash. In front of the main array, several dark figures moved. Theo spotted two guards in gray uniforms. Then a narrow, erect form stepped back from a central screen and shouted into a Victorian-style speaking tube. Immediately a second, portly man appeared from a stairway below and gave a slight bow. Unmistakably, it was Dr. Saint and Mr. Nicely. Theo felt an almost physical pang of dismay at seeing them.

Dr. Saint stood over the controls, like a captain at the wheel of a ship. From time to time he shouted orders at two huge Foundlings, both muscular powerhouses stripped to the waist. Their hulking bodies were covered with tattoos. These human titans, glistening with sweat, were easily the scariest people Theo had ever seen. They were using all their might to turn massive control wheels.

Theo was staggered to see his sober, straitlaced guardian presiding over such an extraordinary scene. What did it mean? What could Dr. Saint be up to? And most importantly of all . . . how could it be stopped?

Theo assessed their chances. The enemies he had already seen, plus a figure at the door of the Otis shaft, made seven foes. That was encouraging—seven was not a multiple of the dreaded three. Maybe they could still stop Dr. Saint somehow.

*The enemy thinks I'm out of the way,* Theo remembered. *None of them suspect how close the Candle Man is.* But did Magnus have a plan? Or were the others waiting for Theo to do something?

Theo was aware that an impatient Magnus had crept up behind him and was peering at their foes too. The old man was fiddling with something in his coat pocket. *Not that brown bottle of smelling salts,* Theo hoped. It was usually a sign that Magnus was about to collapse into one of his wheezing fits. Now would not be a good time!

Theo's thoughts were broken into by the sound of a familiar, arrogant voice.

"We are on the brink of a new age!" Dr. Saint declared. It was hard to get a clear view of him, but it seemed to Theo there was something wrong with his guardian's face. Suddenly Dr. Saint sounded annoyed.

"Where is Baron Patience?" he shouted. "And Lady Blessing? This moment should be witnessed by the Board—to be recounted to future generations!"

"Still no full report, sir," Mr. Nicely replied. "I've just asked the captain of the guard about it. Some sort of malarkey in the upper tunnels."

"Malarkey?" roared Dr. Saint. He approached Mr. Nicely with an urgency that bordered on menace. "That's why I keep you around, you dolt—for your precise and useful reports!"

Mr. Nicely stepped backwards and looked down at his own shoes. "Something about a tiger, sir, and some condors. Hard to confirm details. Didn't want to bother you with it now—what with the Liberation, sir."

"Didn't want to bother me?" thundered Dr. Saint. "It's that fanatic, the Dodo! He's out to spoil my victory! How serious is this report?"

"Nothing—nothing to worry about, Dr. Saint," the butler lied. "A mere skirmish—tunnel rights, that sort of thing." Mr. Nicely no longer had the courage to bring bad news to his master.

"Nothing to worry about?" Dr. Saint snorted. "Then why did you mention it? Don't bother me again, you fool!"

Dr. Saint returned to the control station, which sparkled with sinister purpose under its metal hood. A great roar like thunder from the furnace rooms deep below rocked the tower. Red needles trembled at the top of their dials. Ancient alchemical symbols clicked into place on a counting mechanism. The very air trembled with anticipation. Already the elements themselves hungered for the moment of consummation.

Dr. Saint gripped a large iron lever.

"This is it," he said. "No one can say I failed the memory of the original Philanthropist. When I throw this lever, the Liberation is unstoppable."

That sounded pretty serious to Theo. He glanced around to see if Magnus felt the same. Magnus evidently did. Theo could only watch helplessly as the old man suddenly pulled a revolver from his pocket.

"No!" screeched Magnus, leaping from cover. With a deafening blast, he fired a single, deadly shot.

# CHAPTER 25

# SOCIETY ENCOUNTERS

ELP ME!"

There it was again. Tristus had not imagined it. Someone was crying for assistance in the ancient speech—the noble tongue—from the time of the First Moon.

Tristus had been battling his way through these infernal tunnels for hours. He had smelled the dangerous vapors from the Watchtower above, those first telltale scents that revealed the beginning of a massive alchemical experiment. With the murder of Norrowmore, he had already suspected the worst. A dire plot was being concocted by the enemy and might already be impossible to stop.

First the blocked tunnels had slowed him down. Then sealed hatchways had forced him to use all his strength to keep going. Now floods of steaming water made progress almost impossible.

*"Heeelllp!"*

That desperate voice was the first sign of life Tristus had encountered down here. He kicked his heavy form towards the sound. The oily waters simmered as he looked around in the darkness. A feeble spark of light was provided by a cracked fungus globe farther down the tunnel.

*"Heeelllp*, you miserable, selfish, murdering swine!"

Tristus almost laughed. It was unusual to hear the old speech at all, let alone someone proficient in hurling insults in it — while they asked for your help. He swam towards the small, struggling figure, smeared against the rocks of the tunnel wall. A pocket of foul air had been just enough to keep this creature alive.

"Tristus!" gasped the smoglodyte in pain. "It's me — Skun — you know me!"

Tristus indeed recognized the elusive smog tracker. This one had survived the rooftop battle of the night before. Then the smog had addressed him in vile smog-speech. This time the creature had been wiser, using a more respectable ancient tongue.

Tristus could see that Skun's body had been ripped and punctured by some kind of human weapon. That meant there had been a battle down here. Now Tristus had a use for the smog: information.

He inspected the injured creature. Its heart and brain were still intact—they were both glistening through the shreds of transparent skin. Most of the rest of the body had been melted by the alchemical stream.

"Who shot you?" Tristus asked, still in the old speech. If the smog could keep up a whole conversation in the ancient tongue, then he was unusually wise and perhaps worthy of rescue.

"Human intruders. One old man—and . . ."

"And?" Tristus frowned; he was in no mood to be played around with, and he had little time. His first duty was to stop the alchemical experiment.

"Save me first and I'll tell you. I must repair myself—I need good, dirty air. I just have to get out of this flood!"

But instead of helping, Tristus showed his fangs, as if preparing to feed.

"It was the Candlehand!" cried Skun quickly. "The one called Theo. He came this way, not long ago." Skun pointed with a slimy stick of a finger up the tunnel. "Killed everyone—then went that way."

This was glorious news. The boy was still alive. Then the forces of evil were not yet triumphant. The garghoul did not reveal his great delight.

"I can smell foul experiments," Tristus snarled. "What are the foolish alchemists up to this time?"

"They're bringing the warrior garghoul back to life!" Skun cursed. "Dr. Saint is reviving your rotten people!"

Now it was Tristus's turn to curse.

"*Carramash!*" he growled. "The foul *urughoul* are not my kin." Hot drips from the tunnel roof landed on his horns and trickled down his face. "I am an *asraghoul*—of the high garghoul race. They are our bestial ancestors—a remnant of the volcanic age, doomed to act out the violence of their creation. They only seek a leader to point them at some unfortunate enemy."

"Well, they've got one. The one called Saint. A very nice saint, he is. Promising us freedom to be slaves, getting us to carry his chemical muck, block up tunnels, and squeeze his enemies! Only then does he reveal that he's going to awaken those monsters!"

Skun had worn himself out with his ranting. Smogs enjoyed a good moan even at death's door.

"Poor *nilfug*," Tristus said, using the garghouls' own word for the smoglodytes. "Your people never did get lucky! Always the first to start trouble, and the least likely to benefit from it." Tristus began to swim away. "Thank you, wretch, and good-bye."

"Aren't you going to save me?" Skun yelped. "It looks like you've woken right up now—out of your dream. You'll be alive forever in this disgusting Aftertime. You should think ahead"—he smiled bitterly—"you might need someone to eat later!"

Tristus sighed. He tore away the rock that the stricken smog was fused to, carried the wretched Skun to the nearest shaft, and hurled him as far up it as he could, into the dirty air above.

---

The enormous, tattooed Foundling had just finished turning the great wheel in the center of the control array. His task completed, he stepped backwards, away from his position. At that instant, Magnus fired from the observation post above.

The bullet meant for Dr. Saint went straight through the tattooed man's skull, killing him stone dead. Magnus didn't get a chance to fire again. The guard captain spotted him through the mists and shot back, hitting the old man in the arm. The cemetery keeper spun and fell down the metal stairway, tumbling to the operations platform below.

"No!" Sam screamed, leaping down the steps to help Magnus. Moving like lightning, the other tattooed Foundling got there first. Meeting Sam at the foot of the stairs, he charged into him, crushing Sam against the iron railings at the barrier edge. Sam was so dazed, he hardly noticed the Foundling knock the blunderbuss out of his hand, down into the depths of the Well Chamber.

Theo hurled himself down the steps to help Sam. His hands were glowing, ready for action. But this time Theo was too slow. The Foundling brute whirled round and smashed him in the side of the head with a rock-hard fist. Theo's slight form flew into an iron pillar and crashed back to the floor.

"Theo!" gasped Sam. He staggered towards Theo, but a guard appeared from the mists and struck him to the floor with his rifle butt. Dazed, Sam tried to struggle to his feet, but a powerful boot sent him back to the floor. Sam made a final attempt to rise but immediately felt the barrel of a gun in his back.

The guards dragged Magnus and Sam forwards and threw them into the center of the control platform for their master to see.

"What is this?" screeched Dr. Saint. The hot mists streamed around him as he stepped forwards. Magnus and Sam were held at gunpoint, but Dr. Saint was oblivious to everything except the still figure of the pale-faced, dark-haired boy sprawled at the foot of the metal pillar.

"Theo?" Dr. Saint staggered backwards. "But—but how?" he gasped, his mind reeling.

Sam and Magnus gazed in horror as Dr. Saint's face appeared to shimmer. His skin slipped and crawled off his skull, revealing bright pink muscle, a glittering eyeball, and pulsing brain matter. An instant later, his features reverted back to normal.

Mr. Nicely had crouched by Theo's side, as if to check that the boy was all right. But under Dr. Saint's glare, he rose stiffly and took a step back.

"We—we thought he was dead!" the butler mumbled.

Theo stirred; his eyelids flickered, then opened. Looming above him he saw his worst nightmare. Dr. Saint, the man who had ruled over him his whole life, had captured him once more. His guardian's cold eyes lit up with triumph behind his round glasses, and on his thin lips was that superior smile.

Despair clutched at Theo's heart, but he refused to give in to it. *This man will never, ever control me again*, he resolved. *Even if it costs my life*.

"Get away from me, you liar!" Theo cried. But trying to talk seemed to rip his head apart. He pushed himself up from the floor, but he was too groggy to stand. He remained on his knees, his head spinning.

"Miraculously preserved after all your adventures," Dr. Saint observed. "Perhaps the reports are right—you really do have a guardian angel!"

Theo thought of Chloe. She had been the one to get him out of most of his scrapes so far. Maybe she would turn up now with a hundred policemen to save the day. Then he looked up at Magnus, who was clutching his bleeding arm. There was Sam, battered and bruised, a gun at his head. Right now, a happy ending seemed a long way away.

"It—it happened again, sir, by the way," Mr. Nicely quavered, pointing at his employer's face. "You—err, fell apart for a bit. Your brain was showing. Thought you might want to know."

"Silence!" roared the doctor. "I did not ask you to speak!"

"You fool!" Magnus interjected suddenly, peering intently at Dr. Saint. "Your body cells are unstable! What have you done to yourself?"

Dr. Saint looked at Magnus with distaste.

"Are you the head of this rabble?" Dr. Saint demanded. "Did you steal the Vessel away from me?"

Magnus inclined his gnarled old head in proud acknowledgment.

"Never mind about me," Magnus wheezed. "Worry about yourself! You're not a Wickland. You can't have the true power. You must have experimented on yourself somehow!"

Dr. Saint adjusted his tie and gave Magnus a disdainful look.

"After you took the Vessel away from me," Dr. Saint replied. "I had to find another source of power. Then I realized. It was lying there, awaiting me — in the memory coils of the Mercy Tube."

"You — you went in the Tube?" Theo gasped. He had risen to one knee but was still too weak.

"Oh, yes," said Dr. Saint. "It was never built to cure you of any illness. It was to siphon off your power!"

"I know that," Theo snapped. "I've found out everything for myself!" he added proudly.

For a moment Dr. Saint looked taken aback.

Wincing with pain from his wound, Magnus managed to muster a lofty tone.

"The power Theo possesses is one of nature's most sacred gifts!" the cemetery keeper said, seeming to swell with authority. "It cannot be transferred — you don't have the cell structure! Even now, it's eating away at you!"

"Silence!" screamed Dr. Saint. "I have mastered the alchemy of the Philanthropist, and now I have assumed the mantle of the Candle Man. I need fear no one! I alone am the key. History waits upon *me* now!"

"Well, you got it all wrong," Sam butted in bravely. "Theo's face doesn't fall apart like yours does! Your power isn't right." The guard captain jabbed a menacing rifle into Sam's back.

Dr. Saint glowered and returned to the main control array. "Get them out of here!" he ordered. "Baron Patience will know how to deal with them. I want everyone up on the surface now, except Mr. Nicely and the Vessel—he may still be of use."

There was nothing Sam and Magnus could do. They were marched to the elevator by an armed guard. Theo, now kneeling, could only watch them go. He was helpless to act, still on his knees, dazed and weak, with the guard captain pointing a rifle straight at him. Only the weakest of glows flickered around Theo's fingers, so faint the untrained eye would not notice it.

Mr. Nicely stepped across to the guard captain.

"Don't forget," he murmured. "There are the bodies to take up." They all watched in silence as the dead Foundling was lifted onto a stretcher. The body was so enormous it took the other Foundling and two guards to shift it.

"We aren't finished!" Sam shouted from the open elevator cage. He had meant to sound defiant, but his voice was cracked and emotional.

"Oh, yes you are," Dr. Saint retorted, signaling the guards to bring a second stretcher over. "And if you have any ideas of making a last desperate escape, let me show you what happens to those who defy me. This friend of yours met an unfortunate accident."

Theo saw a guard pull back a sheet to reveal a dead body. At first he didn't recognize the pale face, the drawn features. Then suddenly he felt a chill in his soul as he realized it was someone he knew. It was Chloe.

# CHAPTER 26

# THE GOLDEN TIME

THEO SAT ON A CRATE BY THE elevator, Mr. Nicely standing guard over him, a rifle in his hands. The young man watched the elevator rise away into the clouds, his heart pounding, his eyes misted with tears. Theo felt like his whole world was being spirited away from him, the only people he had ever cared about—dead or alive—all removed at one stroke. Somehow he just couldn't accept that Chloe was gone.

"It wasn't the orders, Theo," Mr. Nicely said quietly. "I'm sorry. She was spotted in the upper levels. The guards shot her by mistake. They're all amateurs. Haven't seen proper army service like me," he mumbled, and looked away, unable to face the young man. The pretending had gone wrong. In fact, it had gone so far wrong he was now having to use the truth to try and make things better. It didn't feel right.

Theo didn't reply. Something about Mr. Nicely's words seemed out of place, but he couldn't grasp why. Chloe's death was too big to take in. He knew he couldn't think about her now.

*Your own feelings aren't important*, Theo thought, remembering his years of indoctrination at Empire Hall. *Remember — you are the least important person in the world*. Right now, that thought kept him going.

Suddenly he heard a deep grinding noise as all around the Well Chamber, circular stone covers rolled away from hidden outlets. Boiling streams surged downwards, hitting the mineral drifts below with a deafening hiss. While Theo had been distracted, Dr. Saint had thrown the great lever.

*Magnus said this mustn't happen*, Theo thought. He rose to his feet, but Mr. Nicely blocked his way, giving a cursory nod at the rifle. The pain of rising so suddenly made Theo almost swoon and he fell to his knees, retching.

"I told you life in the outside world would overstimulate you," his guardian remarked, glancing over.

Now Theo thought he was hallucinating, as sparks of light appeared before his eyes. He squeezed them shut, shook his head, and looked again — but the tiny points of light were still there, filling the whole chamber.

"Alchemists call this the *golden* time," said Dr. Saint. "It is a brief, magical state in which miracles can happen. Earth, air, and water have been conjured to do my bidding. I need one final ingredient to complete the alchemy!"

Dr. Saint was now staring at Theo's hands. Theo looked down to see a pale green glow dancing about his fingers, becoming brighter as his strength returned.

"Get away from the controls!" he cried out, staggering to his feet.

Mr. Nicely went to block his way again, then noticed Theo's glowing hands. The butler jumped back, dropping the rifle in surprise.

Theo lurched forward. Mr. Nicely stared at those dangerous-looking hands. He did not try to pick up the gun.

"Stop him, Mr. Nicely! I cannot be interrupted at this critical instant!" ordered Dr. Saint over his shoulder. The crucial time had arrived for his great alchemical work. "Do it now!" he roared. But Mr.

Nicely stayed where he was. It was probably the first time in his life he had ever disobeyed an order, and he stood there, in his shirtsleeves, like a guilty schoolboy.

"Err . . . no, sir," came the reply.

"What did you say, Mr. Nicely?"

"No, sir," the butler repeated, refusing to budge. "He, err . . . melts people, sir. Wouldn't want to risk it."

Dr. Saint stared at Mr. Nicely, speechless. Part of his face dripped down onto his tie.

Theo's spirit rose at this unexpected turn of events.

"I don't want to hurt *you*, Mr. Nicely," Theo said quietly.

Mr. Nicely gave a weak smile. He looked tired and confused. "I always looked after you," Mr. Nicely said. "You know that, Theo." Except the butler could hardly say the word *Theo*—it seemed to choke him.

Theo walked on, straight towards Dr. Saint, his bare arms held out before him, his shining fingers twitching as if beyond his control.

"Stop it!" Theo cried out. "Stop it now!"

Dr. Saint turned to face Theo with a cold smile. "You're too late!" he declared with evident satisfaction. To prove it, he stepped away from the controls. "The process is now in motion."

252

"What are you doing?" Theo demanded. "Tell me!"

"I'm quite happy to tell you what you have failed to prevent," his guardian replied smoothly. "If you have the good manners to hear me out." He gestured grandly all around him.

"You are in a most sacred place," he said. "Over a hundred years ago, the original Philanthropist, Erasmus Fontaine, discovered these secret chambers beneath London. He used them for his experiments. He awakened dark things down here, creatures from the earth's ancient past—the urughoul, warrior garghoul."

Theo listened, fascinated. After years and years of lies, he sensed he was finally getting to hear the truth. Why? Did Dr. Saint believe he could finish him off any time he liked?

"One by one he called them to life, mindless creatures of destruction. They welcomed his commands. He used them as secret assassins, destroying all those who opposed him. Only one man stood in his way—Lord Wickland, the original Candle Man."

As he spoke that name, he looked darkly upon Theo, a look of open loathing such as Theo had never seen before in his life.

"The war between them was terrible. The police

could not control it. They even had to invent lies and legends, like the tales of Jack the Ripper, to account for some of the slaughter on the streets."

Dr. Saint smiled to himself. As he spoke, Theo appeared to be calming down. Perhaps soon he would become less desperate, sink back into being the docile fool he had always been at Empire Hall.

"Lord Wickland won," Dr. Saint continued. "There were no witnesses to what happened, but a terrible slaughter took place here in the network. Your precious ancestor destroyed them all—the Philanthropist and his army. The lifeless forms of the urughoul were found—by me—at the bottom of this chamber."

Theo trembled. Dr. Saint did not know that Theo had seen the garghoul graveyard—but that proved his guardian was finally speaking the truth. Theo stood there, boldly facing his enemy, like a hero ready for a final confrontation. In fact, he felt ready to drop. Every moment he stood there was torment to his punished body. But at last he was getting answers. He wanted to know all the truth even if it killed him.

"The network—" Theo ventured. "You've turned it into a kind of enormous Mercy Tube. I recognize its . . . echoes."

Dr. Saint twitched with ill-concealed surprise. Part of his ear began to trickle down his neck.

"Clever of you to see that," he said. "But no amount of smart guesswork can help you now."

Theo had been trying not to think about his personal peril. He glanced around to check that Mr. Nicely wasn't going to change his mind suddenly and jump him. But the butler stood blank-faced nearby, unmoving, like a man in a dream. The tiny stars danced like a golden blizzard all around them.

Dr. Saint loomed closer to Theo, a cracked smile of triumph on his face. "I will bring the creatures of darkness back! I will free them from their ashy tomb. They will be my personal army. You have not seen a warrior garghoul in action, Theo—their hands can cut a human apart like flint knives."

There was a chill in Theo's heart—utter dismay at this final proof of his guardian's dark, dreadful ambitions.

"Listen to yourself!" Theo cried out in misery. "Is this your kindness? Your good work?"

Tears were trickling down his face, although he did not remember crying them.

"You are young, Theo," Dr. Saint said, now in a soothing manner. "You don't understand the world.

One day you will find out that there is no such thing as law and order out there. There is only the rule of whoever has the most power. That is why the world needs Good Works!"

"It's not true!" Theo shouted. "If your works are so good, why did you have to lie to me all those years? What are you hiding? Why couldn't you tell me the truth—about me being the Candle Man?"

"Tell you the truth?" scoffed Dr. Saint, a cold smile on his blistered lips. "About the monster you really are?"

"The Candle Man was a hero—not a monster!" Theo cried out. "I've seen the old newspapers—been in your secret room!"

Dr. Saint recoiled at this, truly shocked. His skin rippled like a disturbed pool.

"A hero?" Dr. Saint echoed, giving himself time to recover his superior air. "At first, yes. But he had no control over his power. I gather you have used it already—seen its hideous effects?" Dr. Saint brandished his own hand, the once finely manicured fingers now bubbling and bony.

"I have."

"And in your travels, I expect you have met the Eighty-eight?"

"I—I've been there," Theo said.

"Do you know what they are?" taunted his guardian.

"Magnus wouldn't tell me."

Dr. Saint sighed, shook his head, and placed his hands together in his old familiar gesture of prayer.

"The Candle Man created them!" said his guardian. "They were all victims of Lord Wickland. Anyone and everyone who got in the way of his war with the Philanthropist. They all felt his touch. He wanted to melt them, but he knew little of his power and cared even less. It didn't always destroy—sometimes it merely *changed*. All those ghouls and ghosts trapped down there are not dead—they are victims of the Candle Man!"

Theo wanted to shout at Dr. Saint, tell him this was just another one of his lies. But something held him back—a horrible suspicion that this was the truth, or at least a fragment of the truth. Theo had seen his powers dissolve two men. The bizarre way their bodies had been melted was certainly similar to the hideous transformations he had seen in the gulag. He looked at Dr. Saint now and saw his skin dribbling off his cheekbones as he spoke.

"Thanks to your noble ancestor," Dr. Saint crowed, sensing an advantage, "those pour souls are trapped between life and death, substance and dis-integration."

"Like you!" cried out Theo. "If they are the Eighty-eight, then you are number eighty-nine!"

Dr. Saint froze. His skin began to peel from his head with the shock of this unpleasant truth.

"Yes," hissed Dr. Saint, his face a dripping skull. "Like me!"

A loud klaxon sounded from the main array. The ghastly figure, still immaculately dressed in a dark suit, sprang to the controls and pressed a button. A series of alchemical symbols flashed on the main screen.

"Final phase," Dr. Saint said. "I've kept you talking long enough. Now I'm ready."

"Stop!" Theo cried. "Don't force me to use my power!" He raised a glowing hand. To his astonishment, his guardian responded with cold, mocking laughter.

"That is the one thing I *want* you to do!" Dr. Saint said. He gestured at the row of symbols illuminated on the screen behind him. The one in the center was a curious elemental hieroglyph Theo had never seen before, like a letter *t* with a cross at the top. Dr. Saint's eyes lit up with glee as if he was enjoying a secret joke.

"Your power," said Dr. Saint, "*our* power — the tripudon energy — is the final ingredient needed in my calculations. It is the tiny flame that will ignite this whole chamber and fulfil all my plans. Use it, and you will awaken my army!"

Theo wavered. A cold feeling in his guts told him this horrible claim was all too true. *They always know more than we do,* Choe had told him. That was why they had kept him all those years — to use his flame for evil purposes.

He would not let that happen. He would hold on to his cold fury, the way he had held back his hopes and desires every single day at Empire Hall.

"Then I will not use my power," Theo said bitterly. "Not even to kill you!" He stood defiantly before his guardian, his arms folded, hoping he would not pass out at any moment.

"Your plan has failed!" Theo said. "Your power is just a cheap copy of mine — I can see you falling apart before me!"

Dr. Saint admired his own shimmering flesh. It was now flickering with a weak flame.

"My power will rise," he said. "When I use it to kill you!" He leapt on Theo, clutching at his throat with hands of white fire. A blinding aura of green light blazed around the two figures. But Dr. Saint's skeletal fingers could not grip his intended victim. Energy flashed and crackled between them, hardly allowing them to touch.

Theo tore himself free and fell to the floor, his body glowing, his hair a shock of flame. He felt as if he was burning up; the power was crying out to be used, but he would not be its servant—he would be its master. Grimly, he refused to call upon it.

Dr. Saint bore down on him again. "I'll kill you in the end!" the melting man shrieked, pounding the exhausted boy with desperate fists. But Theo could feel no physical pain now, only the searing energy within him.

"It's over!" Theo cried, breaking away and standing tall with his last strength. "You can't beat me. The power won't let you!"

"I feel the flame! I feel the power rising!" Dr. Saint screamed, raising his hands up high.

Suddenly Theo heard running footsteps. He realized he had taken his eyes off Mr. Nicely for too long. He tried to turn and defend himself, but—to Theo's surprise—the butler raced straight past him.

With all his might, Mr. Nicely pushed Dr. Saint over the edge of the platform.

# CHAPTER 27

# THE UNDEAD

RISTUS WAS HIT BY A WALL OF water and swept away helplessly in the dark tide. After his encounter with Skun, he had been seeking an old tunnel that would take him into the heart of the Well Chamber. But now he was caught in the alchemical streams released by Dr. Saint. The garghoul was swirled through a maelstrom of water, rock, and nameless debris—taken on a perilous ride that would have killed any human—until he was finally hurled into the ashes at the bottom of the network.

He struggled to keep to his feet, surrounded by boiling waters. Dark tombstones rose out of the foaming sea on all sides. He saw the great garghoul monument through the mists and realized he was at the resting place of the dreaded urughoul.

Tristus let out a cry of dismay as the darkness all around him began to glimmer, then explode, with the light of myriad scintillating sparks.

"The enemy has achieved golden time!" Tristus gasped. "Then they have won the war—after all these years." Despair began to take hold of him as he saw the gravestones begin to topple, the ominous mounds stir, and dark claws reach up from under the ground.

Startling figures rose around him like the stone idols of an ancient religion. The warrior garghouls were twitching to life, the first wave of power calling them from out of their ashen graves. Tristus felt a chill in his very soul. Just one of these creatures would prove a formidable enemy for mankind. But here, there were hundreds—more than even he had anticipated.

"It hardly matters if I save the boy now," he reflected. "No one could stand against such as these!"

The waters rushed Tristus towards one of the creatures. To his surprise, its huge claw shattered on impact with his own tough hide. The warriors were brittle, their re-creation incomplete.

"The vital spark is missing!" he realized. "So

where is it? What is Dr. Saint waiting for?"

---

The cry of agony seemed to fill the whole chamber. Dr. Saint had fallen from the platform at the top of the tower and plummeted at least thirty feet onto the level below. *Please let him be dead*, Theo thought as he rushed to see over the edge.

A nightmarish sight greeted Theo's eyes. Dr. Saint's body had plunged onto an iron spar, part of the railings that ran round the lower balcony. The great spike had almost torn his body in two. He hung there, like a figure of medieval torture, his limbs jerking strangely.

Theo glanced away, praying for the body to stop twitching. Just behind Theo, Mr. Nicely was staring wide-eyed, his hands still smoking from where he had touched his employer.

"I—I had to do it!" Mr. Nicely whispered, looking shaken to the core. "I knew it—it all went wrong a long time ago. But I—I was helpless to stop him. I just had to wait for the right moment. . . ."

Theo stared down below. It seemed as if the body was still writhing. It was hard to tell—the little lights of the golden time danced maddeningly before his eyes. The forces of the great alchemical experiment were still in motion. Thunder rolled around the chamber.

*"That wasn't very nice, Mr. Nicely,"* came a thin, unearthly voice.

Theo's blood froze. He gazed below. The broken skeleton was still alive, staring back up at them with its one remaining eye.

"You fools!" Dr. Saint screamed. "You cannot kill *me*!"

Theo looked in horror as the apparition struggled to life. Its limbs had been pulled from their sockets, shredded sinew and torn muscle hung from its frame like string and rags. Only a flickering white energy seemed to be binding it together.

"I'm coming to get you," cried the thin voice. "You first, Mr. Oh-So-Nicely!"

Theo and the butler stared, aghast, as Dr. Saint swung his broken body around on the iron spar. He extended a crooked arm to clutch an iron railing.

*Could it be true? Could Dr. Saint really make it back up? Surely he was finished?*

"It's up to you, Theo," Mr. Nicely said quietly. "No other power can do it. It's just you and him now."

Theo fought back a moment of panic as the truth of Mr. Nicely's words hit home. There was nobody to hide behind now, nobody to defend or advise him.

Only he—a true Wickland—could overcome the thing that his guardian had become.

Dr. Saint slowly began to drag himself off the spike that had pierced his torso. He was leaving several ribs behind but didn't seem to notice.

"You're just a child, Theo!" Dr. Saint scoffed. "You were never going to defeat me! You were always too weak—like that fool who wanted to save you: Norrowmore."

"Mr. Norrowmore beat you!" Theo shrieked back. He would fight Dr. Saint's lies with his last breath. "He planned my rescue—all of it—before he died!"

Dr. Saint was hauling his slimy bones up onto the balcony rail, his gangling legs finding footholds.

"Norrowmore was deluded." Dr. Saint smiled with his cracked, crocodile jaws. He was inching his shattered body along. "He dreamt of peace between our warring Societies! I kindly offered it to him!"

"Peace?" Theo gasped.

"We met in secret," Dr. Saint gloated. "He took my peace proposal away to study. How he must have enjoyed reading it—as my poisoned ink evaporated into him and ate away his flesh!"

Theo felt sick. But this final revelation only made him more determined to defeat his foe. He had to do it—for Mr. Norrowmore, for Chloe, for everyone in the Society of Unrelenting Vigilance who had risked their lives to help him.

Dr. Saint was on top of the balcony railings now, poised there like an enormous squashed spider. Theo trembled on the platform above. He had just had a terrible idea.

*If I jump at him now — and cling on tight as we plunge to our deaths — then it's all over. Candle Man and Philanthropist, the ancient battle over forever. The world free of us both.*

Theo's heart quailed. He felt lost and confused. Too much had happened to him in too short a time. *If I die now, I'll never see Sam and Magnus again,* he thought. *Or ever go out on my birthday again — or eat pink cake.* Theo gulped. Perhaps this was it, the sacrifice demanded of a true hero. It didn't seem fair. He had always imagined that heroes got to actually *live* before they died.

*Clang.* He had reflected for a second too long — Dr. Saint had sprung from the balcony and was now crawling up the banister that led to the top platform.

"I did it!" he cackled, his body creaking slowly towards them, up the last flight of stairs. "I fell to my death — and yet I still came back. It is my *will* that drives me now. I am beyond human!"

Theo braced himself for the attack, but the skeletal figure sprang past him and fell upon the terrified

Mr. Nicely. Dr. Saint gripped the butler by the throat and began to squeeze. But Theo got there just in time. He grabbed Dr. Saint from behind and dashed his skeletal body to the floor.

Theo turned to see if Mr. Nicely was all right, then gasped at what he saw. One bony hand belonging to Dr. Saint had been left behind, still clutching Mr. Nicely's throat. In a flash, Theo smashed it away with his fist. It skittered across the platform and lay twitching. Mr. Nicely fell face-first to the floor.

Theo watched with revulsion as his guardian struggled back to his feet, a demented skeleton in a ragged suit. Theo noticed how slowly Dr. Saint's rickety frame moved—his hideous new power was not without limit. Theo had also noticed something else that gave him great hope.

"Death has made me stronger!" Dr. Saint ranted on, glorying in his eerie power. He pointed at his own ghoulish body, but the gesture was spoiled by the absence of a hand to point with. "I am your master," he raved. "I have always been your master! Look upon me if you dare!"

"I *am* looking at you," Theo replied, his voice surprisingly steady. Theo felt no fear, no doubt as he faced his guardian. "And do you know what?" Theo continued. "I've just realized I can see you perfectly.

Just like I can see everything around me. Do you know what that means, Dr. Saint?"

For a moment Dr. Saint faltered; his one remaining eye looked at Theo, uncertain.

"It means," said Theo, "that I'm not being blinded by stars anymore. It means the golden time has ended!" He gestured all around him, as the last tiny sparks winked out of existence.

"You said yourself it was just a brief spell, when magical things were possible. Well, it's passed! You failed to produce the tripudon fire, and now your chance is over!"

Dr. Saint gazed around him in shock, his head almost flying off his scraggy neck. It was true. The air was now clear. Hatred and revenge had blinded him at the crucial moment. His moment of destiny had slipped by.

Theo had been moving slowly towards his guardian. He was now only an arm's length away.

"Good-bye, Dr. Saint," Theo said, his voice suddenly full of command. Now his guardian was trying to back away, but there was nowhere to go. Just the edge of the platform behind him.

"Remember those old newspapers and books —all the tales of Lord Wickland that you never wanted anyone to see? Well, the words from one of those stories stand out in my mind right now: 'Evil melts like wax at the hands of the Candle Man!'"

Dr. Saint aimed a desperate blow at Theo, but the younger man was ready for him. Theo grabbed the bony wrist and held it in his glowing right hand. Sparks flew as the two power fields collided.

There they stood, frozen in combat, as the energy they possessed struggled to assert only one as the master. Theo looked at his former guardian and remembered. He remembered every miserable hour of his lonely childhood. He recalled the wretched nights he had lain awake, terrified of a rare disease he'd never really had. He remembered every vile deed this man had performed in the name of Good Works.

Theo was ready. Beyond fear and anger now, he was sure of what he had to do. With a calm control he had never felt before in his life, he summoned the awesome power within him to come forth.

Dr. Saint stared in terror as his bones were engulfed in a ghostly emerald radiance. Theo raised his left hand, and an explosion of tripudon energy blasted his enemy right through the balcony.

Dr. Saint didn't even have enough body parts left to scream with, as the molten slurry of his body plunged towards the waters below.

# CHAPTER 28

# THE REQUEST

HE ELEMENTS WERE NOT HAPPY. Earth, air, and water had been summoned in their eternal bargain to create life from the ashes of death. But the fire—the rare tripudon flame—had not been present. The vital spark had been missing. And in the depths of the network, in their vast graveyard, the army of warrior garghoul had been invited back from the darkness—to the very brink of existence—then abandoned.

Now the dark waters still seethed, sullen for revenge, seeking the slightest spark to call forth their rage. When Dr. Saint's disintegrating body hit the waters, the alchemical forces recoiled, ripped each other apart, and erupted through the chamber with the force of an angry hell.

In a single moment, the urughoul were blasted into fragments. Minds of ancient malice—unimaginable to humankind—were splintered and evaporated.

The blast rocked the tower in the Well Chamber—one of its walls sheered away and melted into the fires beneath. Leaping flames engulfed the shattered stone. The platform tilted. Mr. Nicely's unconscious form began to slip towards the edge. Theo grabbed at the control array with one hand and Mr. Nicely with the other. There was a rending noise as the stone ruin began to fall in on itself.

Theo strained to keep hold of the butler's sleeve. Through the stinging sweat in his eyes he looked up to see the last fragments of the elevator shaft melt away in the air above him. *There goes the escape route*, he thought. *I'm glad Sam and Magnus made it out.*

But rising up through the inferno came a dark figure on smoking wings. Tristus, the last living garghoul, had spotted two helpless figures trapped among the flames. Swiftly, he swooped down and lifted them in each arm as if they were rag dolls. The ancient creature's heart soared with joy. Yes, one of the figures was the boy. Against all the odds, he had saved Theo.

Another explosion shook the blazing cauldron

below. The Well Chamber shattered, its ancient roof cracked, and stonework rained down. Tristus rose up through the shattered dome and into the darkness of the passages above.

Theo had swooned from the unbearable heat, but soon a cooler air brought him back to consciousness.

*The Something on the Roof,* Theo thought, *it's come back to save me.* Glancing about him, he recognized the main staircase that he and Chloe had crept down just a day before. A lifetime seemed to have passed since then. For a second, he dared to risk the hope: *Does this mean I'm going to be okay?*

Suddenly dark wings blotted out the shaft above them. Tristus was rocked by the impact of an unseen attacker. His wings were gripped by cruel talons.

Unable to defend himself in case he dropped his human cargo, the garghoul began to spiral down towards the great staircase. In moments they had collided with the iron steps. Theo and Mr. Nicely were hurled across a landing. Theo looked up to see Tristus's body plunging back into the fumes below, under the black wings of nightmarish birds. And down the staircase above descended the unmistakable form of the Dodo.

---

On Larkspur Hill, just behind the Condemned Cemetery, Sergeant Crane of the Metropolitan Police and his special-response unit almost leapt out of their skins as the still of the night was broken by an almighty rumble. It seemed to be coming from below their feet, like subterranean thunder.

"What was that, sir—an earthquake?" a young recruit in a padded Kevlar vest asked. There was no time to reply. Crane's lanky frame suddenly stood out in sharp relief, as beyond him, from the cemetery, great plumes of fiery smoke rose up from tombs and drain covers. Marble cherubs were rocked from their pillars. Crooked stones inscribed REST IN PEACE tumbled to the ground.

Crane and his team could also see a rosy cloud arise from within the walled gardens of Empire Hall, just as a power outage plunged the whole mansion into darkness. Sergeant Crane's radio burst to life and a babbled message made his eyes grow wider and wider.

"It's going crazy over at Southwark Cathedral," he told his men. "We're to move in on Empire Hall now."

As the astonished Sergeant raced through the stone angels and smoking crypts of the great cemetery, he grinned to himself wryly.

"Chloe *told* me there was something going on!" he muttered.

◦•❈•◦

"At last," growled the Dodo as he loomed over his captives on the great stairway. "This time you will not elude me!"

Theo was slumped against the wall, a scrawny, bedraggled Caspian tiger crouched before him. Mr. Nicely, still unconscious, was guarded by a single, one-eared Siberian wolf rat.

The Dodo limped awkwardly towards Theo. The old man's cloak was in tatters, and his hook-nosed face was spattered with blood. A hastily improvised tourniquet was bound around his thigh.

"I have fought my way through half the Society of Good Works to find you," the Dodo said. "We have unconcluded matters to arrange."

"What—what's happened to the garghoul?" Theo demanded.

"My trained condors—the formidable *teratorn*—are keeping him amused. Do not fear for him," the Dodo replied. "He is a creature of stone. You, however, are not."

Theo scrambled to his feet. The tiger backed away slightly, baring its gleaming teeth.

"Now, Master Luke Anderson," the Dodo said, "perhaps you would care to introduce yourself correctly!"

Among all his troubles, Theo felt particularly aggrieved at having his ability to make an introduction called into question. After his extensive reading of etiquette, he had always felt it was one of his few strong points.

"It's not easy to introduce yourself, when you don't know who you are," Theo said with naïve sincerity. "I didn't really know my own identity when I saw you last. But now I do. I am Theo Wickland. The Candle Man."

The Dodo winced and his body stiffened, as if he had just taken a dagger blow. His clawlike left hand made unconscious gripping motions, as if of its own accord.

"Theo Wickland, great-great-great-grandson of Lord Randolph Wickland," the Dodo breathed. "Do you know what you did to me?" he suddenly screamed.

"I'm truly sorry for that, sir," Theo said with respect. "I didn't understand my powers at all then. I doubt I understand them any better now."

"Understand *this*, Wickland," the Dodo said, almost spitting in Theo's face as he drew close to tell his story. "I was just a normal man when I first met your ancestor. I was a zoologist and rare-breed collector who trained certain dangerous creatures to be used—for a fee—by the underworld. Assassinations, poisonings, colorful threats, and such." The Dodo almost smiled at the memory.

"I was not what anyone would call a *good* man," he mused. "I may have deserved a jail term of some kind," he said, his face darkening with bitter memories. "But I did not deserve *this*!"

He pulled back his torn sleeve to reveal his gnarled and stunted arm, and jerked a thorny thumb at his own gruesome, birdlike features.

Theo lowered his gaze. It was hard to meet the wretched stare of those sunken eyes. And he could guess what was coming.

"Your ancestor did this to me—your great Candle Man! Shaped me like wax—misshaped me, I should say. With one touch he ruined me for life, gave me the appearance to match my obsession with rare and extinct animals. And he transfigured my cells, so that I could not die like other men, but live on—in an eternity of weariness!"

"But when I met you—" Theo began.

"I had almost cured myself!" Sir Peregrine roared. "With my own potions, my own decades of

276

tedious research. I had at last learned to control my disfigurement—until you came along!"

The Dodo turned away from Theo, his face tortured, his claw clutching at air.

*And now the Dodo is going to kill me,* Theo thought. *Because of what my ancestor did. Because of my power. Because the world cannot afford to have a new Candle Man running loose, spreading fear and misery in his wake.*

This was it. The Dodo lowered his huge head and stared into Theo's eyes. Theo could smell his stale breath, see the trickling sweat dissolving the dark edges of the dried blood on his cheek.

"Candle Man," he said in a voice of utter weariness, "I want you to kill me."

Theo staggered back, utterly astonished. The Dodo stood still, devoid of menace, calm and composed. A tiny bat dropped like a flake of soot onto the rough skin between the old man's frayed shirt collar and his neck, and nuzzled there. The tiger let out a low, dismal, melancholy growl.

"When Lord Wickland transfigured me," the Dodo said, "he affected all my cells. I can age somewhat, yet I cannot die. I should have been dead and gone for many years now. Life has become a sick joke to me—a pointless shadow theater—with no end to give it meaning."

Theo didn't know what to say. Yet in his heart a spring of hope was rushing up. *Maybe I'm not going to die today after all.* That surge of hope was more painful than any of the suffering he had been through in the last two days.

"Lord Wickland was an arrogant devil," continued the Dodo. "He loved to hand out his punishments to those he defeated. But you — I sense — are not like him. You do not find the Dodo amusing, do you?" he asked, shambling awkwardly to parody his own misbegotten shape. "Would you mock me, sir?"

Theo's answer came readily. "I would not — I *do* not mock you, sir."

"That is wise," rumbled the Dodo. "And only you control the energy. Only you can destroy the work of your ancestor and allow me to die as all other men do. After my unnatural preservation I now long for the mystery of extinction." With his claw he caressed the head of the Caspian tiger. "I want to go where my beautiful friends are going," he said. "I beg you, sir — end my horrible existence."

Theo looked gravely up at the haggard, dejected old man, and paused to reflect.

"My whole life," Theo said in reply, "I only saw three people. Those three controlled my every moment. I came to hate that number, and even all its multiples in the three times table." Theo smiled, realizing he sounded a little crazy. "You were Person Thirteen," Theo continued. "Before you, I had only ever met twelve people. When you examined me, I had a feeling that number thirteen might be a lucky number for me. So, Person Thirteen, I suppose you're okay—deep down."

"I am *not* okay, deep down," growled the Dodo. "I'm looking for death, not salvation." He rubbed his thin hair, bemused. "Anyway, how could anyone possibly dislike the number three?" he muttered. "I should have remembered what a peculiar boy you are."

Theo put his hands together in a wise gesture of prayer, then yanked them apart, fearing he should turn into Dr. Saint.

The Dodo awaited his answer.

"I want *you* to help *me*," Theo requested. "Please. Help me understand my power. When I can control it without fear of creating further tragedy, then I will do what you ask—if you still request it. I need to know there will be no more horrors, and only a man like you can help me. Is it a deal?"

# CHAPTER 29

# TRISTUS'S SORROW

THE GARGHOUL CLAWED AT THE creatures upon him—he even flew straight into a wall to crush them between his body and the ancient stonework. Still the *teratorn* raked at his skin, blotted out his sight with their numbers, tormented him with cruel beaks.

And yet they did not really try to kill him.

*This is all delay and distraction,* Tristus told himself, *a tactic to separate me from my charge.*

"Theo!" he suddenly cried aloud. In a desperate maneuver, he swooped downwards. Closing his eyes, he plunged into the raging fires that only he could survive, igniting the feathered creatures upon him like fireworks. Trailing sparks, he soared upward.

When Tristus landed back on the stairway, he saw the astonishing sight of Theo raising a hand in a parting wave to the Dodo, who, with his wounded and silent creatures, passed silently away into the shadows.

◆◆◆◆◆

"Who *are* you?" Theo asked. He was still deep in the network, fires raging below, the surface a long way above. But now, in the presence of the garghoul who had rescued him twice, he felt he must be close to safety at last. Seeing the creature clearly for the first time, Theo was struck by how much like a man it was in appearance. Despite its horned brow, leathery wings, and stony skin, it still looked and felt very close to human.

Silently the garghoul bent down to study the unconscious Mr. Nicely. The creature checked that the human was in no immediate danger of death, then turned to Theo. The exhausted teenager was sitting on the steps, his head bent low, his dark hair wild, a slight smile on his lips.

"I mean, guardian angels don't exist, do they? And you don't look much like a fairy godmother."

Tristus looked grim. His eyes flashed pure blue

281

for an instant, then his face cracked into an unexpected and beautiful smile.

"My name is Tristus," he said. "I am an *asraghoul*, a noble garghoul, one of the high race from the time of the First Moon—an era long before your civilization. I do not usually wish to befriend humans, but you are an exception," he added. "Come."

Tristus gathered Theo and Mr. Nicely up, beat his wings, and took to the air. The smoke was thick about them, and it was time to get away.

"But how—I mean, why are you here?" Theo asked. "Have you been following me?"

Tristus sighed. "First—tell me quickly, what happened below?" The garghoul listened in wonder as Theo related Dr. Saint's downfall. At the end he said nothing, but his smile told Theo that he was deeply glad at the way this day had gone.

"We have been lucky today," he said finally. "Now I suppose I must tell you a little." They were flying steadily up the main shaft, through the levels of the network. Theo was grateful to see the long stairway slip away below him.

"A hundred years ago," Tristus said, "I was the first garghoul to be awoken by the Philanthropist. He found me sleeping among the ancient carvings deep in the network. He thought I would be grateful—an eternal ally! But I had been happy in my stone dream. I never forgave him for awakening me. He sought my help in his war with your ancestor. I, however, chose to side with Lord Wickland."

They had arrived at the top platform. Tristus set Theo and Mr. Nicely down. The butler suddenly coughed, his body jerked to life, and he rolled over onto his side.

"Good," whispered Tristus. "This one is coming back from the brink."

Theo sat on a fungus globe, his throat parched, his eyes sore. He still had so much to ask and was terrified that the garghoul would flit away.

"Why did you side with Lord Wickland?" asked Theo. "Were you friends?" Theo had heard such dreadful things about his ancestor that he longed to believe he was a wonderful figure, lord of ancient mysteries, ally of garghouls.

Tristus pondered long before he spoke. It seemed to Theo that there was a dark cloud on the garghoul's brow.

"Now is not the moment to tell the tale of those times—times so dark I hope you never know their like. But I will tell you this much. The power that Lord Wickland carried—and the power you now hold—is sacred to my people."

Theo frowned. He had seen the horrific effects of his rare gift. This remark from Tristus was, to say the least, unexpected.

"Sacred?" he echoed.

"Yes," the garghoul replied. "It was recognized in the Beginning Time and called *tripudon*."

"That's what we call it!" Theo said.

"Because you are using our language when you do," Tristus retorted. "It is the energy of the *jump*— the power to change things. It is the force that brings life to a stagnant world." The creature's beautiful eyes glimmered brightly and seemed to fill the dark tunnel with starlight.

"In this cold universe it is the difference between *yes* and *no*, the reason life takes its chance over the barrenness of death. Theo, you have scarcely begun to understand your power. It is precious, and it will grow with you—as your wisdom grows. Use it well."

Theo noticed that Tristus had grown gloomy again, his head hung low. He wondered what made Tristus so sad. Was it because he didn't have the power? Did he miss his old friend, the original Candle Man?

"Lord Wickland *was* a hero, wasn't he?" Theo asked.

"Yes, he was," said Tristus. "And he was also terrible. Exactly what was needed in his time."

Theo must have looked dismayed, for Tristus lay a consoling hand on his shoulder.

"Your ancestor was a great man, Theo," the garghoul said. "You have a proud history to live up to."

Theo smiled. He had always believed there would be something good about his terrible destiny. He had known it in his heart all along.

"And you want to help me, because I'm the new Candle Man," Theo said, comforted.

But the garghoul's eyes darkened to midnight blue. "It is not as simple as that," he replied.

"Then why —?"

Tristus interrupted. "Just because you can ask a question, it doesn't guarantee that it has a good answer," he said mysteriously. "Or an answer that you would like to hear. Now, enough questions!"

Tristus supported Mr. Nicely and helped the delirious butler to stagger along the passage. They were heading slowly upwards now. Theo felt he could almost smell the surface air.

They had reached the hatch. Memories began to flood back — of the last time Theo had stood at this secret doorway, and who he had been with, before the terrible events of the last day. He drove these thoughts away and, like an old campaigner, hit the central plaque lightly — *tip, tap, tip*.

"This is as far as I go," Tristus said, helping Theo support Mr. Nicely on his own young shoulders.

"So, will I see you again?" Theo asked. "There's so much more I want to know."

The garghoul rose into the air.

"If you are lucky, you will never see me again," Tristus said. "For that will mean you never have need of such a — a friend." The garghoul flitted away into the shadows, and it seemed to Theo that the creature had been striving to conceal tears in his voice.

Theo was left in the vault beneath the cathedral, shouldering Mr. Nicely towards the world outside.

———

As he staggered towards the open cathedral door, Theo heard sirens, shouting voices, a distant helicopter. In the surface world it was three o'clock in the morning, and a damp, dismal night. Unnoticed, Theo half fell out of the doorway and saw a courtyard filled with policemen, Foundlings under armed guard, someone carrying a dead condor.

And he saw Sam — though Sam didn't see him — standing by an ambulance. Next to him was Magnus, lying on a stretcher, with an oxygen mask over his face. Theo collapsed to his knees and let Mr. Nicely roll off his arm onto the freezing ground.

Then Theo heard someone call his name. At first he didn't recognize the voice. It seemed to come to him out of a dream, from behind a door that should be forever closed. Then he saw someone running towards him, a big happy smile on a familiar, wonderful face. Beyond all hope, he fell into the arms of Chloe.

# CHAPTER 30

# MILLET AND GREENS

THERE WAS A LITTLE OLD man in a brown suit and burgundy waistcoat running around getting in everyone's way. He had a pink, well-fed face and short hair like fine silver wire. He carried an old leather briefcase and a pile of papers.

"My name is Mr. Sunder," he piped up. "I need to speak to someone!"

Sergeant Crane turned him round with two firm hands and propelled the little man back out towards the hallway.

"Speak to someone, then," he said, "but not me!"

Empire Hall had been turned into a temporary operations center by Inspector Finley. The immense

Scotsman, in his perfectly tailored dark blue suit, beamed with delight as his men turned Dr. Saint's private study upside down. Already he knew he was sitting on a gold mine. He wanted to make sure no secrets were overlooked, and he was determined to keep the investigation as need-to-know as possible.

Several Foundlings were under armed guard in the hallway. The Mercy Tube had been cordoned off behind white tape and sported several colored stickers saying HAZARDOUS MATERIALS. Veracity, the new maid, was sitting on the floor in her nightgown, crying.

The dining room had been taken over by a special mobile medical unit. Mr. Nicely, who was needed for his inside knowledge of the Hall, had already been bandaged up and taken into the study to make a statement. Theo was lying on a foldout bed, with a fracture mask on the left-hand side of his face and a tube sprouting out of his arm.

"What you really need," said Chloe, passing through with a report for Sergeant Crane, "is a haircut—you look ridiculous." Theo's adventures had left his dark mop standing on end, and it showed no sign of wanting to lie back down.

Chloe soon came back to sit next to Theo. She was wearing her familiar navy greatcoat, with saggy camouflage trousers underneath.

"Sounds like I missed everything." She sulked, sipping Theo's glass of water. "You selfish lot! Storming Dr. Saint's secret base without me! Sam told me all about it."

"What happened up here?" Theo was dying to know. "I've been rushed around in a police ambulance; fussed over left, right, and center; forced—by you—to give a statement; but told next to nothing! Tell me or I'll explode!"

"Coming from you, that's entirely possible," Chloe joked. "So I'd better do as you say."

Theo listened with astonishment to Chloe's tale. She'd had no trouble escaping from the network, then a complete nightmare trying to mobilize the police. No one except Sergeant Crane seemed to believe anything she had to say. Finally, Inspector Finley had been reached at his club at about midnight.

Finley was shown the bag of evidence and went ballistic. He sent one squad of men to Empire Hall and another to investigate the secret passage under Southwark Cathedral.

"When we got there, it all started happening," Chloe said. "I didn't even have to show Finley the hatchway. Walking wounded started pouring out of the crypt. Society of Good Works people—engineers, soldiers, Foundlings. None of them had weapons and most of them had weird bites and scratches. They didn't have any fight left in them."

"The Dodo strikes again!" Theo grinned.

"Shush!" Chloe said. "We don't need to tell the police everything!" she whispered. "You know what that lot are like."

Theo *didn't* know what that lot were like, but he was pleased to hear Chloe talking about the police as *them* instead of *us*.

"Seems like our pal Sir P decimated the Society of Good Works while hunting for you."

"So what about — ?"

"Sam and Magnus surfaced with one of the groups." Chloe grinned. "The creatures hadn't attacked *them*. The enemy was so demoralized after being pummeled by the Dodo's forces, they didn't even have Sam and Magnus under guard anymore. I just explained to Finley who they were, and we called an ambulance for Magnus. Sam insisted on going to the hospital with him. They are both going to be okay."

"Why aren't I in the hospital?" Theo asked, glancing at his drip-tube.

"The Mysteries must be respected," said Chloe, with a glint in her eye. "I persuaded Finley that you shouldn't be examined by conventional medicine, so there's a special police team here. Also I didn't want to let anyone as disaster-prone as you out of my sight! You see — unrelenting vigilance." She grinned. Then her brow knitted in amused concern. "I'm still not quite sure what bit of your report to let old Finley see. Don't answer any more official questions — unless *I'm* asking them," she added.

"But what really happened to you?" Theo pleaded. "I've asked you about a hundred times. I thought you were dead! Was it just a trick of Dr. Saint's?"

Chloe looked grave. She laid a gentle hand on Theo's arm.

"I've been trying not to tell you," she said. "You're in such a state already." She sighed and took Theo's hand.

"No, it wasn't a trick," she said finally. "It was Clarice."

Theo felt a sudden lump in his throat. He blinked stupidly.

"Clarice?" His head swam.

"After she helped rescue you, I told her to run away and keep her head down. But she was worried about me — and you. She turned up at Crane's police station, but they turned her away. So she remembered one or two things I'd shown her over the years, I suppose. She found her way into the network at the Monarch Fields end. Got shot —" Chloe paused, her feelings welling up.

*Clarice. Chloe's twin sister.* Theo had forgotten all about her. Miraculously, he now had Chloe back, but he had lost another, dear friend. Chloe took Theo's gloved hand and held it tightly. He tried to say something, but words would not come. Kind, sensible, calm Clarice was no more. While he and Chloe—the ones who had been in the center of all the danger—had survived.

"We've got the guard who did it," Chloe said. "Not much left of him anyway, after those rats had a bite of him."

Theo didn't care about the guard. He had just realized something—and solved a mystery that had puzzled him before.

"That explains it," he gabbled. "I thought it was weird that Mr. Nicely apologized for you being killed. He didn't even know who you were! Dr. Saint didn't either. He thought he was showing me that Clarice had been caught and punished!"

The excitement of this realization passed and turned to misery in his heart.

"Poor Clarice," he mumbled. He was recalling all those times she'd looked after him, plumped up his pillows, brought him his hot water with a sympathetic smile. He remembered the desperate nights he had poured his heart out to her, when she couldn't hear a word he said but just soaked up the sadness he was feeling.

"She's the real hero in this," Chloe said quietly. For a moment, neither knew what to say. Then they hugged each other and cried and cried.

# CHAPTER 31

# CONSEQUENCES

T WAS MIDDAY. Theo had slept for several hours. Injections had taken all of the feeling out of his broken cheek, and he had been dribbling on his pillow. He sat up in bed. Every bit of him that hadn't been injected hurt.

The calm, the silence, and the solitude were nice. Theo looked around the old dining room that had been converted into a ward. He had never been in here before. The shiny mahogany paneling was much more splendid than the bare old room he had lived in. He shook his head, wonderingly, at his guardian's endless deceptions. Now all over.

For a moment he felt a pang of regret for the

passing of his old life. What was it today, Thursday? On a Thursday, round about now, he would usually be sitting in his room, staring at the shadows on the wall, or looking through his favorite book — *Woolcombe's Bestiary of Postdiluvian Extinctions* — while waiting for Clarice to bring him in a glass of warm water.

Compared to a life of panic, alchemy, smogs, and slaughter, his old tedium seemed almost desirable. But now, Clarice was dead. There was no one to bring him water anymore, and no one left to force him to drink it. Everything about his life had changed forever *Scary.*

There was a knock on the door. Sergeant Crane, in his hideous brown suede jacket, opened the door to admit Mr. Nicely. Chloe followed. The annoying silver-haired man, Mr. Sunder, tried to sneak in just behind her. He was repelled by Sergeant Crane, who dragged him away down the hall.

"I have a perfect legal right to be here . . . ," the man continued, but his muffled voice soon disappeared in the distance.

The room fell silent. Chloe came and sat next to Theo. *Still defending me,* he thought to himself.

Mr. Nicely held up his bandaged hands. "I've been discharged by the doctor," he said. "But I, err . . .

don't think the police have entirely finished with me."

"Not by a long shot," said Chloe.

Theo looked up at the butler with a wan smile. Mr. Nicely's torn waistcoat was hanging off him and he seemed to have lost weight.

"They, err . . . said I could come and see how you were," Mr. Nicely said, "before I go off for questioning." He hung his head. Theo looked at the man he had known all his life, as if he were seeing his face for the first time.

"You saved the day, Mr. Nicely," Theo said. "If you hadn't turned against Dr. Saint —"

"Don't," Mr. Nicely said sadly. "I don't deserve any commendation for anything I've done." He pondered for a moment. He looked older; his chubby face was sagging, and his cheeks were speckled with silver stubble.

"What made you turn against him in the end?" Theo asked.

Mr. Nicely considered deeply, then looked at Theo with clear, sad eyes. "Well." He sighed. "I've been given a lot of orders over the years, mostly stupid tasks given to me by stupid people. But right at the start there was one order that stood out: 'Look after Theo.' That was what the Society of Good

Works asked me to do. And after all the years, and after all the rubbish I had to do, that was the one task that really meant anything to me."

He looked down, embarrassed at the sentiment he didn't usually show. "'Look after Theo,'" he repeated to himself with a tired smile. "Best orders I ever had."

"Thank you," said Theo. "I'm glad you decided to follow them—in the end."

A policeman quietly entered the room and nodded at Chloe. Mr. Nicely sensed his time was up.

"It's all a bit of a mess now—the Society of Good Works," Mr. Nicely said quickly. "But when I— when I get out, I'll be glad to come back and help out a bit . . . if asked, I mean."

"That would be good," Theo said. "Whatever's left of the Society might be good for something one day, I suppose. Maybe you can be in charge of pretending everything is all right all the time," he added with a faint smile.

"I hope to, err . . . give up the *pretending* lark and be a bit more useful than that," Mr. Nicely replied. "If there ever *is* a next time."

At a nod from Chloe, the policeman led the butler away. Theo watched him go, the last one of the Three who had once ruled every instant of his life. Instead of feeling happy, he felt anxious, cut adrift.

As the door was closing, the annoying little man nipped through.

"Theo Saint?" he asked nervously.

Theo looked up in surprise.

"Who are you?" Chloe groaned.

"Don't worry, I've satisfied Inspector Finley that my legal presence is required," he said, seating himself in the most comfortable chair in the room. "I'm Mr. Arnold Sunder, solicitor for the Society."

Theo closed his eyes and lay back. He had finally had enough.

"Do you have to do this now?" Chloe asked.

"Oh, absolutely," Mr. Sunder replied. "There are wheels — shall we say — to be set in motion!"

"What wheels — what motion?" Theo sat back up.

The little man opened a leather-bound file. "We've *heard*," he said simply. "And I'd like to offer my condolences for the death of your guardian."

Theo didn't know what to say.

"We thought you should know, as soon as possible, sir, that Dr. Saint made no special provision for the incidence of his own sudden demise. Nothing in writing at all. So under the circumstances, you being his ward . . ."

Chloe's eyes suddenly widened, and she quickly suppressed a smile.

"Err, yes?" Theo prompted, still puzzled at the intrusion.

"It actually means, sir, and I hope you'll be in some way comforted to hear, that *you* are now the Master of Empire Hall."

"I—I'm what?" Theo gasped.

"If there's anything you need, anything you want—anything at all—you only have to say the word." The little man beamed.

Chloe clapped Theo on the shoulder.

"Congratulations." She grinned. "Theo, you are the new head of the Society of Good Works."

Theo groaned and buried his head in his pillow.

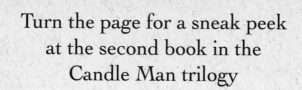

Turn the page for a sneak peek
at the second book in the
Candle Man trilogy

# CANDLE MAN

BOOK TWO

## THE SOCIETY OF DREAD

Coming from Egmont USA
in Fall 2010

# CHAPTER 1

# A WALK

*How hard can it be?*

Theo had never been for a walk before—on his own—but he was pretty sure he could do it. He hunched deeper in his big winter coat, feeling the January chill. The wind ruffled his lank, black hair. Cold air sparked tears from his gray eyes. He shivered—he was not used to being outside.

*Don't panic,* he told himself. *Thousands of people go for walks every day. You can do it!*

He took a deep breath and surveyed the dismal, damp street before him. In the past, he had been allowed only one walk a year, planned by his guardian Dr. Saint. Now, Dr. Saint was dead. There was no one to tell Theo what to do. In fact, he could do anything he liked.

That was scary.

Theo looked back at the dark shape of Empire Hall, the vast mansion in which he had spent his whole life. Since the death of his guardian, he now owned the great house. It was one of the biggest mansions in London, but the sight of it brought Theo no pleasure.

*I've never owned anything before*, Theo thought. Owning something was also scary.

His cautious footsteps had brought him to the Condemned Cemetery, the graveyard that backed onto his house. Dusk was just beginning to gather among its tombs and woodlands. Theo liked dusk. It had always been *his* time, after the chores, routines, and dreary activities of the day were over. In his imagination, anything could happen at dusk.

An old man, walking slowly with a big stick and a plastic earpiece, headed towards him. Theo panicked. He considered turning back—then remembered the words that he needed.

"How do you do?"

The old man frowned at Theo, grunted, and moved on.

Theo's heart was pounding, but he was happier

now. He had faced a tricky encounter, but his book, *An Introduction to Introductions*, had saved him.

*When meeting a stranger or new acquaintance, the traditional greeting of "How do you do?" is all that is required,* the book stated.

The wrought-iron gates of the cemetery were open, a thin mist covering the ground within like a gray sea. He stepped inside, all senses alert. His long coat dragged through the wet nettles and overgrown weeds.

Theo peered around, focusing on the stone grotesques and angels with fascination. He knew from experience that such things could come to life. But nothing like that happened now. In fact, on this drippy, slow January day, the world seemed quiet and empty of excitement. Dead.

That was just how Theo liked it.

Turning back, he could see the lights were being switched on in Empire Hall. It was hard to believe that all the business of the great household was going on without his presence.

A strange sensation stirred him from within. It was a feeling he barely recognized: freedom.

It was wonderful to know that the dark adventures he had been plunged into were over, and now he could start living a normal life—for the first time. It was delicious to breathe the damp air and smell the strange scents of the overgrown cemetery. He walked through the rows of tombs, gazing at every weathered stone carving, solemn inscription, and tattered funeral bouquet. For someone who had never been taken to a scenic view, park, or public garden, this graveyard was a world of wonders.

*Just a bit longer,* he told himself as he ducked under the ragged hawthorn trees and ventured deeper into the cemetery. Theo saw a narrow, almost invisible pathway between holly trees and followed it, taking delight in the sparkling cobwebs among the dripping thorns, the bright red berries, and the brown-and-golden ferns, curling in the chilly air.

*This is a magical place,* Theo thought. *I wish I could wander here forever.*

Suddenly, he glanced down at his hands at the leather gauntlets he wore at all waking hours. A pale, green light was flickering from his fingers. He frowned. His power was stirring. That was a sure sign of danger . . . but why now?

"At last!" boomed a voice, interrupting Theo's thoughts. A giant figure broke through the holly bushes and loomed over him. The man was dressed in a vast leather coat, his throat swathed in a checkered scarf. His skin had an exotic, yellowish tinge and old, wine-dark tattoos could be glimpsed on his powerful hands. "You don't even know who I am, do you?" the figure snarled.

Theo held his breath but tried not to panic. He didn't need to know who this was. He just had to find the words.

"How do you do?" Theo blurted out quickly.

The man lashed out with a big leather boot and kicked Theo's legs out from under him. Theo cried out and crashed to the floor, almost fainting from pain and shock.

"How do I do?" growled the man. "How do I do, when you and your Society of Vigilance friends shot my brother and ruined all our plans?"

Theo's mind raced. He *had* seen this man before. The tattooed man was a Foundling, one of the ruthless army that his evil guardian had unleashed for his own dastardly ends. Theo's hands were buried deep in nettles and, unseen by the attacker, he began to work off his gloves.

"Well, it's all over for you now," the man sneered. He paused, eyes glinting, savoring Theo's plight. "*He's* back," the man said with a nasty smile. "And he's more powerful than Dr. Saint ever was. He's back and now you're finished!"

*He's* back? Who was *he*? Theo wondered as he tried to edge away.

"They told me you was special—you had some kind of magic," the Foundling said. "Well, I've never seen it, and I don't think you'll have much when I've pulled your heart, lungs, an' liver out."

The great tattooed man moved in on Theo, who was desperately scrambling backwards through the weeds. Now that Theo had taken his gloves off, the nettles were stinging his skin.

"Well, I escaped the police, didn't I?" the man said. "I've hidden out and watched and waited for a chance to pay you back."

He wrenched Theo from the ground and swung him backwards, preparing to dash Theo's head against a gravestone.

But the Foundling never got the chance. He felt the faintest touch, just the slightest whisper, as the trailing hand of the frightened boy made contact with his cheek. The Foundling couldn't move. He stared down at his own body, which was glowing a luminous green.

Theo fell to the ground. He edged away as he watched the man's skin bubble and smoke. Then, the angry, frightened face of the attacker slid downwards, a gaping skull shining out from the ruins of the flesh.

With a whooshing *hiss* the man melted into a big steaming pool.

"Theo!"

Theo had climbed on top of a stone tomb to avoid being touched by the hot slime. Through the bushes came a familiar figure in a navy greatcoat and pulled-down peaked cap.

It was Chloe. She took in the scene, clapping her hands to her head in dismay. "Theo—you idiot!"

---

The dark bookshelves towered above them on both sides as Theo and Chloe sat together on an old leather sofa in the library of Empire Hall.

"His name was Jim-Jack Kip," Chloe said, still huddled in her enormous coat, even though they were now back indoors. "That is, if I can rely on your colorful description of the assailant. The police have been hunting him for weeks."

There was a slight twinkle in Chloe's eye as she said this. Many years of lonely, miserable imprisonment had made Theo observant of the tiniest details, and his description was sure to be accurate.

"You're barely well enough to be going out at all," she said, her brow knitting in frustration, "let alone going out without anyone keeping an eye on you!"

Theo peered through the back window that opened onto a little courtyard. It was now dark outside. His breath made a cloud of mist on the pane, and he childishly drew a gloomy face.

"I thought it would be all right. I thought all the trouble was over now."

Chloe frowned. "Don't be dense, Theo! Look, I'm a member of the Society of Unrelenting Vigilance. It's my job to watch over you! You might at least help me a bit by telling me when you're taking a stroll with a tattooed assassin!"

Theo couldn't help but smile. "And I know you also have to protect me because you're in the police."

Chloe sighed. "Yes, someone in our secret society thought it would make me twice as useful to the cause. I suppose I'm a kind of double-agent," she said with a grin.

"And I'm double-protected," Theo replied. Now that Chloe was there to joke with, he was already starting to forget the shock of the attack.

"But you're the Candle Man now. You have enemies — people who don't want an old crime fighter from Victorian times to come back to life! Dr. Saint may be dead, but he had allies, armies of villains at his command. I tried to make a list of your possible enemies last night, and guess what — I ran out of paper!"

310

"Ha-ha—good one," groaned Theo.

"I'm not joking!" Chloe said.

Chloe looked thoughtful. "He is back," she said, musing on the words of the attacker. "That's what's bothering me. If only we knew who 'he' was . . ."

Suddenly, she jumped up.

*Wait!* she mouthed at Theo. She put a finger to her lips and, in a swift movement, she darted to the library door.

Theo watched. The doorknob was slowly turning. He crept to Chloe's side. They held their breath as the door creaked open.

"Down!" Chloe nudged Theo, urging him to take shelter behind a bookcase.

A lumbering, dark form appeared in the doorway, accompanied by clinking and rattling.

"Hot cocoa, sir?" boomed a deep, warm voice.

It was Montmorency, the new butler, reversing in with a rolling cart. Chloe sighed and flopped back down in her chair.

"Bring it on," she said eagerly.

"You see," Theo said with a smile as the butler departed, "things aren't always as scary as they look."

"Well, things are pretty bad," Chloe insisted, helping herself to some chocolate fingers. "But there's one thing we do have on our side: you."

Chloe wiggled her fingers in imitation of Theo using his powers. Theo sighed. He didn't like it when she did that. He sat back and sipped his chocolate.

"We've also got you," he replied. "So, I'm sure we'll win in the end. Don't worry, Chloe. Dr. Saint is gone. I escaped from Jim-Jack Kip. The bad old days will soon be over."

Chloe frowned into her steaming mug. "The bad old days are never over."